Scrums

and

Bananas

Enjoy
Hannah x

HANNAH EVANS

Wuggles Publishing,
Clydach, Swansea, South Wales.

Copyright © Hannah Evans
July 2010

ISBN: 978-1-904043-19-5

Any questions, contact
scrumsandbananas@hotmail.co.uk

To the late Chris Caswell (Piano Man), whom without, this novel would have never been written.

And

To Alan Tudor Jones, my mentor, my friend.

ScRUM AND BANANAS

HANNAH EVANS

KICK OFF
Scrums and Bananas

Chapter One

As if buggering off wasn't enough, my prick of a father has buggered off and got engaged. But not even just engaged to a bird my mates might fancy, Oh no, that knob head that provided the sperm to create me is sodding engaged to a fella! A bloke, complete with cock and testosterone.

'Meet Mike,' the prick had said like it was the most natural thing in the world. 'We're getting married.'

'Oh right that's nice,' I said. I mean, I was convinced this was a bloody wind up. My Dad wasn't a bender, I mean, he'd taken me to the rugby for years, been force feeding me halves of cider since I was about eleven, never touched me other than patting me on the back in that manly fashion dads did once their sons came off the rugby pitch. And here he was introducing me to not only a boyfriend but a bloody fiancé. *Mike* the fiancé for Christ's sake!

He'd taken me to a café to tell me the "important news" One of those trendy places that are ten to the dozen in Cardiff. Foreign music playing, fairy lights on the ceiling, everything on the menu at least three quid. The waitress, who brought us two decaf cappuccinos and a large coke, 'cause they didn't do pints, was mega smart, the type of bird my dad would have flirted with over the bar at the rugby club a couple of months back.

Funny really I hadn't noticed the missing 'Cheers babe' and that now really sleazy wink that I had tried to master as a child. At the time I was a bit curious to whom the lad that looked like a valley's replica of Beckham was. I wondered why dad was hanging about with a boy who was five years older than me, decked out in cheap silver, sparkly earrings in both lobes and had obviously had one too many sun beds. His T shirt for Christ sake looked like it was from the kid's section and his hair must have taken absolutely ages.

And then they hit me with it, and as I said I thought, trust dad to pull this out of the hat. Then that fucker Mike touched my dad's knee and they were grinning at each other like bloody idiots. Just sat there, in front of everyone, smiling.

'It's really good to finally meet you and I'm glad we've got your blessing,' the poofter squeaked at me. 'I hope we can be friends?'

Uh? No chance mate. Not in this lifetime or any other. Gob-smacked, I wasn't giving them my bloody blessing. Absolutely gob-smacked. And then a sickening pain that remained with me all over the summer holidays started. The mankey unsure-ness of myself, my dad, the thought of the explanations that would have to be given to the boys at school, the rugby lads... Oh god the rugby lads. What the fuck was I going to tell them? "By the way boys my dad's now gay and engaged to a bloke but don't worry its fine."

I kept thinking about Kelly Thomas who was in my registration class when I first started comp. She was really fit. All the boys would have hard-ons in P.E over her gym shirt. Then last year, it came out her mother was a dyke! A real one! She'd kicked her old man out and shuffled this really hard looking bird into her house. Needless to say, Kelly went from Top-Totti to Minger during a lunch hour, all because of her Mam. I mean, that was going to be me if I let this horrendous news get out, not that I'm Bloke Totti or even that popular but at least I had normality under my belt. Just one look, just one quick glance at the sodding lovebirds told me this was going to be difficult to hide.

Chapter Two

When he first left, I was twelve. It was December. Mam was bawling her brains out as he carted his hold-all down the stairs. I supposed it was crammed with his essential shit. She was crouched on the hallway floor as if someone had died, groaning and moaning like the cat had when it had kittens. I was in the living room mindlessly watching TV, pretending to do homework as he wandered round claiming random stuff, like the electric thermometer that was in the window, some early Christmas cards that decorated the mantelpiece and the salt and pepper from the dining table. What the fuck did he need the salt and pepper for? It still baffles me; I mean, he didn't even like pepper!

As he left he ruffled my hair and said, 'Be good kiddo.' the twat didn't even cry, and be fucked would I let the tears slip out whilst he was there. What a cock.

A few weeks later I found myself in Mam's car outside an ugly block of flats.

'Go on love,' she had said. Her eyes were puffy and swollen. 'He's still your father.'

He was on the nineteenth floor and as I ambled up the stairs, delaying my journey by analysing the graffiti on the walls, I wondered whether we'd have crackers? These worries were easily confirmed. After twenty minutes of staring at the door, I bit the bullet as they say and walked in. I've got to be honest the vision of my father's bare arse thrusting through the air into Leah, the barmaid from the rugby club on the kitchen floor, wasn't exactly what I had expected.

'Oooh, baby!' she squeaked in her stupid girly voice.

'Hiya, Dad, Merry Christmas.' There was a lot of fumbling and swearing as they composed themselves, but I didn't hang about for the wanker to explain. Bugger that for a laugh. Straight back down the stairs I was.

So three years on the fucker's engaged to a bloke who looks nothing like that slut Leah from the club and he wants me, me his son to be mates with the daft twat.

I wasn't left with many options. I didn't want to completely disown the bloke. Yeah I hated the prick for what he had done to my Mam, but at the end of the day, he was my father. The fact he'd acquired a boyfriend who he

7

plans to marry was just completely out of the question. He'd been shagging a seventeen year old GIRL a couple of years back and now he's almost levitating into tight jeans, plucking his eyebrows and wearing a pendant for Christ sake. I had to ask what was the world coming to?

The valley I live in was still coming to terms with the fact the vicar of Saint Mark's church had run off with Mrs Ford, the landlady of the Crown, leaving the Vicars wife and his devoted congregation completely speechless. Never mind two fellas tying the knot. I'd be known as the freak whose dad loved cock. God, what if people thought I was a bender?

Chapter Three

Telling my Mam was the second strangest experience of my life, the first obviously being, my Dad telling me he had decided to become gay. I waited for her to finish her shift at Tescos and she came in as she always bloody did, bitching about Amanda from customer services, the beep of the till and in detail, every customer that had 'intensely' annoyed her during the one till six shift. I nodded in agreement with a sympathetic look on my face as she switched the kettle on, put the shopping away and emptied the dishwasher all at the same time. Fair play. Since he left she'd become a machine, three years of this routine I'd had, three bloody years of tears, unpredictable moods and compulsive cleaning and now I had to tell her this.

'Mam, Dad's getting married.'

I couldn't see her face. She was facing the plate cupboard. I did however see her frame start to shake as she gripped the unit for support and the moment before she turned around I swear to god I could have killed the bastard for doing this to me, to her. What sort of a bloke was he for Christ sake?

'Who to?' she whispered. She was panting and her face was pale as hell despite the fake tan Aunt Mary had spent slapping on her all of last night.

'Who to?' her voice hardened as the news sunk in. Oh God what the fuck was I to say? Three years on and the bastard still has an effect on her.

'His name's Mike. He's about twenty.' I don't know why I felt it necessary to tell her his bloody age. I mean it doesn't matter how old the poofter was. He was a bloody man, an XY chromosome for Gods sake.

'What are you on about?' oh she was confused alright. Her face must have been the exact picture of mine when he told me. Except mine being male, with no make up etc, etc.

'Who the bloody hell is Mike and what's he got to do with your father getting married?'

'Dad's marrying Mike, Mam.'

At first I thought she'd lost the plot, because laughing hysterically really wasn't what I had expected.

After the giggling stopped the tears started and she got straight on the phone. Not long after the screaming began. I can tell you if I used swear words like that to her I'd be grounded for the rest of my life! She was probably as shocked as me. They'd been married for thirteen years before the divorce. Mam had got pregnant with me and Nanna and Bamp made her marry him. She said they'd been in love but the day he left I heard the wanker say he'd never really loved her.

Mam was asking, "How fucking long?" and "Who was the bastard trying to kid?"

As selfish as it sounds I really couldn't take anymore, I'd heard enough. This shit had been going round and round my head for the last twenty four hours, I was as upset as her, so I wandered upstairs and blasted my stereo to block her ranting.

To vent my anger in an appropriate way I started forcing myself to write continually with my right hand. Probably could have had a more fulfilling evening but I swear to god

9

my brain was twisted to turmoil and back. I of course am left handed, and so is knob head and I'm trying to eliminate everything I've inherited from him. I've also decided when I go back to school, to stop having the expensive stuff from the canteen at dinner times in order to save my lunch money for a nose job. I've got his nose see. I'm sure Marion the dinner lady would notice though but it didn't matter, soon everyone would know.

'What's up with you babes? No cheeseburger today?'

'No Mar, I'm saving my lunch money for a nose job cause I've got the same one as my old man and as he's completely mortified me by getting engaged to a bloke, I know longer want to be associated with the fucker.'

Of course really I'd say:

'Nah, I'm off meat to be honest, Mar.

Chapter Four

I'd been thinking about getting my hair cut for ages. I was gonna go for the Gavin Henson spikes but *Mike* had had his hair in a similar style so my final decision was to have it shaved. Oh yes a numero uno I do believe. The thugs of the estate all have shaved heads under their counterfeit baseball hats, originally from Turkey, imported to Digger Dave from 'Costa-Del' Merthyr Tydfil. 'All yours for a fiver a piece.' After I'd been to Steve the Barber's I'd definitely place my order for a hat.

'Whose dad has come out?' they'd say.

'Couldn't be. His son has a shaved head and a hat.' Wink wink, nudge nudge.

Steve must be about three hundred years old now. He'd been cutting generations and generations of male's heads in the valley. He knew my Dad and both of my grandfathers and probably their grandfathers too. His shop always smells of old spice and he always wears a dickey bow. His takings are kept in a bum-bag and he strongly believes the internet is technology of the devil. Of course, of all bloody days when I could have done with a manly chat, I had the bloody second in command, Davy. Not that I've got anything against Davy, he had been my next door neighbour for years, always did my hair tidy. He knew my dad and my parents divorce details because his Mam had looked after me during the whole procedure. But, he was a weird herb at the best of times.

'What do you think of homosexuals, Davy boy?' I enquired. I mean, I had to get to know what people thought, had to be aware of who was going to lynch me when they found out and all.

'I fucking hates them, along with Turks, Jews, Vegetarians and fucking old people. Can't stand wrinkleys man.'

'Wrinkleys?' I wondered whether we were on the same wavelength.

'Yeah you know? They shuffle around bitching about the youth and the fucking war and *it wasn't like this in my day* shit. Hurry up and die then you whining bastards. And another thing why do they save all their bloody food. Even the mealiest scraps. Whoop! In the fridge they go *no fucking waste in my house lad.*'

'Yeah but gay's? What do you think about them?' I veered the conversation back on the original track.

'Well, wouldn't float my boat. Not natural is it? Another dick up your bum. I mean a finger's bad enough; I've had the finger twice. Once by Doctor Sinah but I was only about eight so it didn't count, and once in the shower. Lathered up and all, and as I was cleansing the nether regions, as you do like, my finger slipped up there. Oh I whined like a bitch alright.'

I decided on a trim.

Chapter Five

Four days after his big confession, which was like a week into the summer holidays for reference. The sound I had

11

been dreading echoed through the hallway, bouncing off the kitchen tiles, where I was making a comforting peanut butter sandwich and ringing through my ears and all around my brain.

The telephone's shrill bell stirred an uneasiness in the pit of my stomach, and it took me about eight rings before I mumbled a feeble *hello* into the receiver.

'Jonno! Alright, kid?' it was Wedgy, my captain. He play's second row, a massive boy with blue eyes and fluffy blonde hair. Mr Griffiths our history teacher reckons he'd have been Hitler's prototype if he'd been about then. Lucky he wasn't mind, imagine that, 'Hitler, buddy. Fancy a pint?'

Wedgy has a tendency to chase skirt, as Mam puts it. He also likes to shake his monstrous dick through the steamy air of the changing rooms after a win. This was a phone call I really didn't want. God, I hope he hadn't heard.

'Alright boy what's up?' good start I felt.

'Well JJ it's the presentation on Friday...' shit, bollocks, bugger, shit. The presentation. A Friday night filled with jugs of cider, testosterone, dares and the girls from year eleven that have fake ID. Great Stuff.

'... and the general consensus is that Meeky buys us a bottle of Vodka before hand, cause we know that prick will get served, and we keep it in the pans so we can have shots in our pints to get us, you know? Shit-faced. So you owe Meeky a fiver.'

'Alright yeah cool.' Phew.

'Oh and my old man asked was your Dad coming cause your Mam's coming, she phoned my Mam yesterday?' shit.

'Uh. No he's not coming. He's staying in Cardiff.' I stopped there. If I started lying now God knows where I'd end up or what I'd get myself into. He's in a play, (too gay) he's got a date, (too risky) he's broken his leg, (too stupid.)

'Alright I'll let him know then mate. We're meeting up behind the changing rooms at quarter to six so we can determine the plan of action like. So I'll see you later JJ, Ta-ra.'

'Ta-ra Wedge.'"

Then I was sick all over my mother's wooden floor, and there was nothing I could do about it. It was as if someone had turned a tap on at the back of my throat and all the misery and shame poured through it in the form of my breakfast, lunch and tea of the previous four days. What was my Mam thinking of for Christ sake? I bet she'll get pissed up and tell everyone fuck face has become a bender.

How the hell was I going to relax if she was guzzling white wine smearing the glass with that mankey brown lipstick she'd first bought when he left.

After she had found out about the barmaid and once she stopped whining and her face had resumed to its normal shape, her eyes not swollen and that funny red mark that spreads over her skin when she's cried had gone, she planned a night out on the town with Wedgy's Mam.

She bought a new lipstick. It had been like a stand, y'know? The new women kind of thing. I remember the night she had first gone out as a *singleton* (her phrase, not mine). She came back with Wedgy's Mam holding her up on the one side, Maureen who worked the same shift in Tesco as her, on her other side and some woman with a perm and lots of gold jewellery carrying her handbag and shoes. She was bawling and her make-up had left black like slug trails down her face. She was whining and slurring about being thirty-one with no husband exedra, exedra.

This is what would happen on Friday if she was let loose at the bar, but this time it would be in front of all the lads and all their parents and fuck knows who else. Can you imagine Saturday? The valley, the terraces twitching with the scandal of a newly out fudge packer.

We were eating a very depressing tea of burnt sausages and lumpy mash when I decided to bring it up. It had taken me ages to clean up my spew. That's the thing with wooden floor isn't it? It's slippy and difficult to clean so I just ended up moving it about. To say I was really pissed off at this point, would be an understatement. I was seething in my own misery and anger and there she was ignoring the fact her ex-husband, my Dad was engaged to a man and our whole future, our family reputation was at possible risk by her attending my shitty youth presentation. Alright. We hadn't had a bad season but it hadn't been fantastic either. We'd finished the league fifth in the table and had the Binxy youth Memorial Award under our jockstraps but there was no real need for my Mam to be present. That is, unless the club were desperate for another mortifying Karaoke version of Abba's *the winner takes it all* that Mam dedicated to 'That fucking scrubber behind the bar' at the Christmas dinner?

'Mam. We need to talk,' tactful with not a trace of bitterness in my voice I promise.

'Look, Jonathan, not now. I've had a shitty day, no, no I've had a shitty life and I'm eating shitty mash and I really don't want to think let alone talk at the moment so don't OK?'

And that was the end of our chat.

Chapter Six

The next day something awful happened. Dad's parents, my Nan and Bamp, turned up at the house. Luckily Mam wasn't in work until seven, so when they arrived at ten past eight in the morning I knew I wouldn't have to be alone with the crazy bastards.

My Nan loves lager. That's all anyone has to know before meeting her. Oh yes and she's been on anti depressants since Princess Diana died. My Bamp, an incredibly placid bloke, mumbles a lot, shuffling around after *Crazy Nan* (a name I labelled her when I was old enough to realise).

'Ooohh it's just bloody, bloody awful.' she blew her nose into a woollen handkerchief she had knitted during a Baywatch repeat.

'I can't believe it.'"

These gestures of complete amazement went on for quite a while, so did the blowing of her nose and quick nips out of a hip flask which was no doubt filled with Stella Artois, or possibly banana schnapps.

I know this because last week she sent me up Digger Dave's with a brown envelope and he told me his boys would be back from France with the van tomorrow and what was my Nan's order again?

'Oh yes, half a ton of Stella and three bottles of the Schnapps, be there tomorrow, late afternoon kid.'

An array of green bottles now take up residence under their stairs and an equally impressive array of empty bottles decorate the path at the back door, ready for recycling.

'I never knew, he never said, see? Did you know lurrvy?'

I saw Mam's face drop. Nan was plastered. Of course Mam didn't bloody know, she married the prick. I really don't think she would have made the vows if she knew he was batting for the other side.

'There's something, I remember when he was a babi. He wouldn't stand up to wee. Said Mary sat down to wee so he wanted to. I should have guessed then.' was this a valid confession you ask? Well I would have said it was pretty authentic if Nan hadn't been talking to the bloody plant pot, the fake Yucca at that.

'Not normal is it? I thought he'd grow out of it but if he insists on marrying this *whatshisname*? That man, you know, he obviously still has a wee sitting down.'

Oh good god, no wonder Dad's turned out weird if this is Doctor Nan's diagnosis for why he's suddenly started fancying men.

'Perhaps it was something we did Alf? I knew you shouldn't have encouraged him to move to the city. It's bloody rampant down there, *homeo-sexuality.*' she whispered the word like the pronunciation was contagious.

Dad had moved to Cardiff about six months ago. For those of you who don't know, Cardiff is in the South, like the valley I live in, although technically the Valleys are the South-East, but anyway, Cardiff's about a forty minute drive from my house. Nan's only been to the City three times in her entire life. Once when her and my Bamp took me down for my twelfth birthday when she managed to point out every Welsh celebrity she knew of. It would have been quite sweet to have seen the glamorous whirlwind that is my crazy Nan exclaiming that Tom Jones was in the frozen food isle of Marks and Spencers or that Shirley Bassey accidentally hit her with a carrier bag in Next, except the unfortunate shoppers that bore a slight resemblance to the actual superstars (As in, Tom look-a-like was male and the Shirl had brown hair.) had been terrified by Nan's booming theatrical tone which certainly made sure every other shopper in the capital was aware that obviously old Shirl' and Tom were aimlessly shopping unaided by an entourage.

There were security guards and even a police car involved.

I really wanted to point out to Nan that *homeo-sexuality*, as she says, in fact is not just rampant throughout Cardiff, but the nation and even the fucking world. God, if only she knew the truth about George Michael. I mean it'd break her heart but the woman needed to be told...

'I mean how do they have intercourse? Close your ears JJ Bach. Where do his bits fit in? It's just not possible is it?'

Mam had her face in her hands and her body was trembling. The news was a raw cut and she didn't want to consider the technicalities. My throat squeezed into my neck and my heart rate was just like one of those shit hard house nation tunes that Davy always plays. I can feel the vibrations of the records through my bedroom wall sometimes and that's how my chest felt through my T-shirt.

'NAN! Stop it.'"

She focused her sparkly eyes onto my face. She couldn't quite look me in the eyes, probably because she couldn't focus on the four of me that stood in front of her.

'Look here Buddy. Don't ever raise your voice to me again. Who do you think you are?'

Time out! I love it when adult's put this ball in my court. Who do I think I am? Well I'm Jonathan Jones, fifteen years old from Ebbw Vale, South Wales, U.K, Earth. And at this precise moment in time I'm Jonathan Jones whose father's engaged to a fellow male of his species and my Nan's considering how they're meant to have sex. So quite frankly I'm very aware of who I think I am. Of course these thoughts spun through my head way to fast to phrase so I came up with; *drum roll.*

'Fuck you.'

'Jonathan!' my Mam gasped more than shouted and I was glad it wasn't a shout because I'd swore for her benefit. Nan had been crucifying her with all those nasty details. I didn't hang about to see how much shit I was in exactly. Just walked through the front door (slamming it for effect) and wandered down to the pitch, where once again I spewed my ring, only this time I had to use my fingers to help it along my swollen throat.

Chapter Seven

My Rugby Club's ground is called Deri Cross Park. At the far end of the ground or at the rear entrance, whichever way you want to look at it, is the valley's cricket club so technically there are two fields within Cross Park. The senior squad used to be in the premier division but the Welsh Rugby Union came in and re-arranged the league and basically the club were left with bugger all.

We used to have boys that went from mini to senior then played for Wales when we had money but that's all stopped now. The terraces in the Park are where the minions stand (They were once voted the most aggressive terraces in Rugby World Magazine). They're really basic and when I say basic, I'm talking concrete steps and metal bars with no shelter whatsoever. The toilets consist of four concrete walls and a drain, and stink of old, dry piss. Opposite the terraces is the stand where the committee, sponsors and Gold vice president season ticket holders sit but that's no classy establishment either.

The flip down plastic chairs are either broken or don't work and you're lucky if you get one a bird hasn't shit on. The walls of the stand are covered in names and love hearts drawn in black marker by pupils past and present of my comprehensive. When you hit year eight you qualify to hang about in the stand on Friday (well we're not supposed to) and Saturday nights with bottles of cheap cider. We (as in, me and the boys) hang about in the summer sometimes but during the season its pointless 'cause we can't drink on the Friday and Saturday after the game we get served in the club.

The day I swore at my Nan I sat on the terraces. I'd love to say I was contemplating or even being deep and meaningful, but truthfully I'd blocked all thoughts and was just enjoying the sunshine. I love the sun. When I was eight, when things were normal, we went to Lanzarotte for a week. It was Mam's idea. That was like the beginning of their rough patch because I remember her telling Auntie Mary, who's not actually an auntie, I'm not sure why I call her Auntie Mary, although at Christmas and birthdays she always sends me money, on the phone that it'd do them both good to get away. Anyway, we flew from Bristol. It had been the first time I'd been to England, first time I'd been to an airport and the first time I'd been abroad.

That holiday had been perfect, our family unit was perfect and I was sure there was something magic about the sun. It made people carefree and happy. Mam ate ice cream, something she never did in Wales and Dad got up and sang 'Delilah' on the karaoke, stood on the hotel bar, dancing and he didn't shout at me or Mam for the whole seven days.

Two weeks after we got back from Lanzarotte Dad walked out for the first time and it kind of became frequent behaviour after that. Things were never tidy again, not after that holiday.

It was the way the sun sort of tingled on my skin that reminded me of Lanzarotte as if little spiders were crawling through my freckles (that at fifteen I was yet to rid although Kaleigh Adams from my English class said they were sweet, I personally think Kaleigh Adams herself is sweet, but each to their own I suppose). The terraces were quiet, just normal outside sounds decorated the hazy air. I was comfortably warm and I was happy in my memories and I was quite tired.

'JJ boy what are you doing up there?' I jumped.

'What am I doing up here? What are you doing on that contraption?'

It was Steve the Barber.

Steve dismounted the lawn mower and bounced up the terraces. For an old bloke he was dead fit.

'Know George the grass? Well he's buggered off to Tenerife with the Mrs. I drew the short straw to tend to the bloody pitch. Thought I'd be easy didn't I? Being the summer and all, totally forgot its peak season for the poxy cricket, and they got a big game tomorrow. Anyway back to my original, what are you doing up there on your own JJ? Everything alright?'

'Not really Steve.'

Course I knew Steve was the key to most of the valley's secrets. Everyone confided in him. He was wise and gentle with his advice. You felt as if he really cared about your welfare, which I think he did. So, I replayed the horror that had become my life Steve patiently shook his head and

19

nodded when necessary and wiped his wrinkled brow with both understanding and as if he was considering every aspect of the story for a worthy solution.

After I finally got it all out I felt as if I'd had my guts ripped out of me. My voice was quivery and my hands shook but I felt my body was loads lighter seeing another human being's reaction.

'Oh hell boy, you have been through it, haven't you?'

I was afraid to answer this question because I could feel the shame prickling at my eyes. Steve's face was so friendly and understanding I wondered if he could just make it all better. He would get something magical out of his shirt pocket and make everything go away like in films when the old dude turns out to be a wizard or something equally as cool.

'Right boy. I'm going to tell you a story now that could make you feel a little bit better, or bloody terrible, OK?'

I nodded. Back to the real world Oh Christ what crap was about to worm its way out of the woodwork.

'When you Dad was a boy, about your age in fact, he had a friend, Brian Moore his name was. And JJ the two of them were inseparable, God, till they were way into their twenties. Anyway, the village always had their suspicions, like they do.' Steve rolled his eyes. "But the two of them always had girlfriends, no one serious, but nevertheless girlfriends.'

I was beginning to wonder where this was going.

'Then one day they just stopped bothering. Neither of them giving any clues to why, just stopped being friends. Brian moved away not long after and soon folk forgot about him. Your Dad married your Mam a couple of years later so people assumed that the two boys had just been *friends.*'

OK. This is where it got complicated.

'JJ, do you understand what I'm saying? They had a very special friendship. A relationship even? OK, no one knew exact details but those boys had a bond. And perhaps your Dad, now, has finally found his way?'

Right. That's what the old boy was getting at.

'So you mean he never loved my Mam?'

'I'm not saying that, Boyo. Course he loved your Mam and he was besotted by you when you came along, but there's many forms of love Jon, you'll find that out.'

'I'm not gay!'

'I know you're not kiddo but you don't have to fancy someone to love them.'

He tapped my shoulder and as he got up his old, wise bones clicked and cracked. I was grateful for the chat like, but where the bloody hell did this leave me now? Knowing that my parent's marriage had been based on a lie and that I should be happy the prick has finally found his bastard way, Jesus I would have bought the knob an atlas for if I'd known.

Chapter Eight

I once read that if you eat too many bananas you can die of potassium poisoning and if you are really unlucky and pick up a banana with high potassium you can die from eating that one banana. But how do you know if every time you pick up a banana that particular banana doesn't contain like, too much potassium? Really there's no way of knowing is there?

My Mam going to the presentation is like picking up a banana and asking myself, 'I wonder whether this will kill me or not?'

Chapter Nine

On the Friday morning of my presentation night I wrote one thousand lines with my right hand saying 'write down all the things that you want to say.' It's lyrics from a

Stereophonics song. It's off their first album and I've got to be honest, my right handwriting has improved into the realms of fucking not bad since my Dad told me he was queer. So, when I met the boys behind the changing rooms, under the stand my right bastard hand was in agony.

'JJ ya skinny minge where's the puppy fat gone?' Meeky's our full back. He's got really black hair and loads of stubble, he looks a bit like an Italian my Mam always says. He usually has about four girl's texting him and we all kind of, I dunno, worship him I suppose, in a completely non-gay way, mind.

'What are you on about?'

'You have lost a hell of a lot of weight JJ.' Wedgy piped in and all of a sudden the whole squad were eyeballing my physique.

'Can't say I've noticed,' I said

'Have you been dieting?'

God, what was this, the third bastard degree on my eating habits?

'Oh well, skinny minge, get this down ya neck.'

I've got to be brutally honest with you at this point. Never in my entire life had I drunk vodka before and seriously if I had, my eyes would have watered by just looking at the big glass bottle Meeky handed me. So you can imagine the effect it actually had, when I did neck it straight back from that same glass bottle. I coughed, I cried a little but most importantly I carried on drinking. And for those of you who haven't consumed vodka it's really quite an unpleasant experience. Take it from someone who knows. The effects are not 'bloody marvellous' whatever your team mates say and whatever you, yourself may think at the time.

Chapter Ten

By the time we sat down for dinner I was steaming. We were allowed to get served at the bar but only pints, which was a bit of a bugger because I was getting a taste for the old vodka. Anyway, I was sat next to Meeky which was ideal to be honest, as I had a perfect view of my Mam. I tried my hardest to lip read her as she chatted to the boy's Mams, as if nothing was wrong, like. I watched her pouring the white wine down her neck and laughing, which was very worrying. She hadn't laughed in a long time.

'What's up with you boy?' Wedgy's Dad was our main coach. I'd always got on with him. He was one of my Dad's closest friends and I couldn't help wondering, as he placed a pint in front of me, what he would think if he knew. Knew, my old man was having it up the bum?

'Nothing Adrian, just a bit tired.'

'Alright boy, as long as you're OK.'

I spent most of the night heading back and fore the pans to take advantage of Wedgy's plan. And the plan worked a treat until Dingo, our forwards coach, clocked on to how half his squad couldn't form a sentence and continued to only use the middle cubicle. It was way too late for him to do anything anyway as we were all shit faced. I had started to relax, right about the time the presentations stopped. We'd had grub, which was a minging version of Sunday dinner and started playing drinking games with some of the senior squad when it all started to go wrong.

Cowboys and Indians verses lager is always a lethal game to play after a meal with gravy, but this game proved to be particularly messy. I was sick in the Binxy Memorial cup that we were previously using as a punishment jug. (The loser of the game being forced to drink the concoction out of the cup, made by Alun Jones, club captain.) Wedgy had shit himself, literally, and had to wear a pair of old shorts that had been left behind the bar years ago and Meeky had totally lost the ability to speak.

So, as you can imagine I had completely forgotten about Mam. Well, that was until I saw her gyrating round Kieron Davies on the dance floor. Kieron Davies is a centre in the senior squad although he's only nineteen, that's fourteen years younger than Mam, for reference. He's also played for the district, county and bloody country. He's currently waiting to hear whether he'll be singed by the Ospreys (Swansea's team) for next season, so he's one cocky bastard. Just so you can get an ideal image of the boy, he's naturally blonde, unnaturally tanned with sort of turquoise coloured eyes (I only know this cause my auntie Lisa is obsessed with him, so don't go thinking I'm a bender, right?).

There was some sleazy song playing via DJ Bunny, the local idiot who thinks he's the valley's version of Judge Jules, and I could hear the boys chanting and you can guess the rest. Me being properly pissed for the first time in my life and slightly confused to why my Mam had Karin's tie on her head and was dancing in a way I'm to embarrassed to describe lash out in the only way I saw to be appropriate after a quarter of a bottle of vodka and around about eight pints of cider. Was there a fight you ask? Did I attempt to lamp Kieron and brandish my Mam a tart? Oh no, I was sick, again, only this time behind the radiator, then nicked the raffle prize, a tasty dessert wine, apparently, And I got passed the stage of inebriation, oh yes I'd say even passed paralytic. In fact, I got completely wasted, fell asleep, and lost two whole hours of my life.

A couple of clues did emerge to what might have happened the following morning. For a start I woke up on Wedgy's floor with Debbie his Spaniel, on a blow up bed thing. I also had the player's player trophy under my pillow, which would suggest I won it. Or stole it? There was also a text message on my phone that read:

WAY HEY PLAYER GET IN THERE KALEIGH ADAMS HAS BIG TITS. MEEKY.

But, it was when I stumbled to Wedgy's kitchen that my hangover really kicked in.

'How's you feeling babe?' Wedgy's Mam.

'A bit rough to be honest, Mrs W.' me.

'Adrian will run you to the hospital now, if you like?' Wedgy's Mam.

'I'm not that bad Mrs W.' me.

'Don't you want to see your Mam babe?' Wedgy's Mam.

Perplexed was my expression.

'He can't remember, can you?' Wedgy.

Everyone looked perplexed, even Debbie the spaniel.

'Babe, do you remember?' Wedgy's Mam.

'Remember what?' me.

'Oh God. Babe, your Mam took a fall last night on the way home. Banged her head. Quite badly. She's down the hospital.'

Oh Christ. How the hell had that happened? I don't even remember leaving the club let alone Mam falling. Shit what a mess.

'Is she going to be alright? How come I didn't go with her?'

'They wouldn't let you go. You were a bit worse for wear kid. Don't worry, Adrian went with her. He said she's fine they stitched her up and kept her in for observation because of the amount of alcohol she'd consumed. But I'm sure they'll discharge her this afternoon, Babe.'"

Chapter Eleven

They say bad luck happens in threes don't they? Well bloody hell that's an understatement judging by the goings on of my life. Firstly, my Mam's ballerina pirouette outside the club caused more damage than initially thought. I'll be honest, it took a few days for her lunacy to register but I'm blaming it on being stressed up to my eyeballs.

She started setting four places at the dinner table and muttering in the kitchen. Neither offences that suspicious really. Four at the dinner table is a nice even number and

25

who doesn't at times chat to themselves whilst enduring mind numbing tasks like preparing spag bol?

The moment I realised something was really wrong was when she pulled up on the drive, in not her crappy British racing green citron but a golf buggy. I watched her unload the buggy, struggling with full Tesco bags. Oh hell, had she been to town on that contraption?

Bollocking downstairs at the rate of bloody light I was mildly alarmed to see Mam putting jars and jars of peanut butter in the cupboards wearing one of Digger Dave's baseball hats strategically placed sideways, V new kids on the block I must say. (Yes I do watch 'I love the eighties' on VH1).

'Alright, love?'

'Erm, yeah, what's up Mam?'

'Whadewemean?'

She'd moved on to another load and was now putting the same vast quantities as the peanut butter of cherryade into the fridge.

'We're not usually allowed pop.'

'I know wicked en' it? Wicked? Wicked? Where in God's name had she bloody been?

After a couple of attempts in restoring normality into this bizarre situation I asked her was she feeling alright.

'Who the hell are you?'

At first I thought she was insulted by my concern, but taking in her startled expression I realised she was really messed up.

She then started to rant at me in some sort of foreign language. She looked possessed if I'm honest. Confusion, on my part was not the word.

'Mam?' now, this is where it started to get really strange.

'What does he want? Who is he Eric? Do you think we should eat him?' she seemed to be talking to her shoulder.

The doctor came just after she tried to stab me with a bread knife. He sedated her, made me a cup of tea and

26

arranged for me to stay next door with Davy's mob. He than admitted Mam to the nut house. Marvellous.

Some would say my second batch of bad luck would be staying next door while Mam got better but it turned out Davy's was a minor endurance compared to what was to be.

Chapter Twelve

I was well aware Davy's craziness stemmed from Mrs Taylor or Julie as she told me to call her but I wasn't quite prepared for the mayhem of number fifteen.

'Come in babe,' she said as the call out Doctor ushered me through their front door. All ready being de-briefed by the GP Julie chirped on constantly at her normal rate of chatter and then alarmed me slightly by dropping in:

'She'll be fine in there boy, God, even I've done a stint in Hedges Mental House. Lodsa' fun, doll.' she giggled.

The Taylor's house could easily be a museum for tack. There was clutter and cheap shit everywhere. Christmas shops got nothing on their place I can tell you. Julie has dyed red, curly hair, wears an immense amount of pink floral outfits and reeks sickeningly of make up and perfume. She addresses everyone as *babe* or *doll* or *chick* and even drinks her tea out of plastic cocktail glasses. Their religion is Coronation Street and displays of Weatherfield's cast, past and present proudly decorate most of the house. A signed Ken Barlow has prized position on the mantel piece.

A put-me-up bed was installed for me in Davy's room with a duvet cover of no other than Thomas the Tank Engine which Davy was a little stroppy about, as his was a mere patterned number.

Davy is tall and lanky with floppy unwashed blonde hair. His voice is deep and mellow as if he's on 'go slow' constantly. He could easily be thirty odd but I think he's only in his early twenties. If you wander up our street early morning when the sun's out you'll often find Davy putting his time off to good use attempting to make patterns out of the dew on his mother's front lawn.

'Seen some dude on Blue Peter doing it see, so, I know it's possible.'

He's constantly pulling up too big trousers that sport sporadic stains of God knows what that have decorated his clothing from, I can only suspect, the early eighties. His T shirts probably from about the same era, are emblazoned with phrases such as, 'I LIKE VAGINAS.' So when I tell you after my first restless night at number fifteen I was given a bowl of Smarties floating in milk for breakfast you'll find it of no surprise.

'And how's our JJ babes this morning, ey?' Julie breezed around the kitchen in an oriental robe, her mass of red curls contained by a silk eye mask that covered her forehead and eyebrows.

'Oh I'm alright thanks, em, Julie.'

'Sleep alright, doll?'

'Yeah thanks.' no point mentioning Davy's constant wanking and jibbering kept me up.

'Good. I got some news anyway. Your Dad's coming to get you in a bit to take you to see your Mam.'

To be honest with you I hadn't really taken in what she'd just said. I was in fact, attempting to work out whether she sounded more like the current land lady in Coronation Street or the religious biddy out of Eastenders. Whichever accent she was trying to master really clashed with her welsh twang.

'Oh OK.'

'He's bringing, erm, Mike is it?'

Mike? Mike? MIKE! Shit, shit, shit. I had been so wrapped up in Mam going mental and residing at the Taylor's I'd totally forgotten the cause of all this mayhem. Prick features and puppy bollocks.

'He sounds like a nice chap, lovey. Your Dad couldn't work his hands free on the mobile so he said they'd be here within the hour. Told me all about the wedding. You must be quite excited?'

Of course I couldn't answer her I had to bolt to the pan to spew. And spew I did boy. Chunks and lumps of my misery and Smarties poured from me once again as reality hit home.

Let's take a look at this from the referee's angle shall we? Oh yes, definitely the sin bin for JJ's Dad. Thoughtless insensitive bastard.

Just as I looked up from the bowl to a large photograph of the king himself, Tom Jones, that hung lopsided above the bog, the doorbell went. Well, the theme tune to Neighbours belted through the house along with a 'Ooohh isn't that marvello!' from Squeaky balls.

After I'd splashed my face with cold water and had sworn at my reflection several times I ventured down the stairs. The topic of conversation was my Mam, and my Dad's tones floated towards me from the kitchen and instantly anger flared within my insides. I'm not sure how it formed itself, cause I was pretty calm until about the fourteenth step of Davy's stairs but then what I can only describe as a silent fury took hold of my reins until we were in Dad's BMW, where I let rip.

On reflection I bet Mike the pansy thought I was the one that should have been in the nut house. But God, where did these pair get off trying to be involved? Spreading their smarmy secret as if it was something to be bloody proud of. Sick it was, fucking sick.

I screamed and shouted, ranted, kicked and punched the whole twenty minute drive to the hospital. If I hadn't all ready guaranteed a first class ticket to hell my language in the car had guaranteed it.

Chapter Thirteen

Where Mam was hospitalized was kind of idyllic if you could forget it was, well, what it was. The hospital itself was an old building, the type of ancient house that's in the rude films Nan watches, where women wear big dresses and fan themselves and stop breathing when the totti comes along on their ponies. Its gardens, which are huge and covered with flowers of all colours and neat grass, have no dog shit and only fallen branches litter the lawns. Squirrels squirm and leg it as soon as humans, visiting or on release from their wards, wander about, and who can blame them.

Think Christmas weather, think frozen ponds, numb skin, red noses and that pretty much sums up the atmosphere in the waiting room as Dad, Mike and myself sipped cheap coffee from polystyrene cups.

'I love the décor, dead gloomy.' Mike, I think was attempting to defrost the atmosphere.

'Not now OK.' my Dad spat, which made me kind of like him, momentarily of course. Mike pouted, Dad paced, I frowned.

'Hi, I'm Doctor Atwood.' A guy in casual clothes with a name badge and clip board, the only signs of professionalism, shook all our hands. 'I'll get straight to the point. We're all men here.'

I half grunted, half laughed.

'Christine's behaviour has been brought on by a build up of stress. It's a rare case and we haven't quite got to the bottom of it, as cases like this are quite extraordinary. All her faculties are intact but she's having problems getting them to function with her behaviour. Now, I have to ask is there anything that could have triggered this off? Moved house perhaps or a bereavement?'

'Well, Jon here said she took a fall last Friday, couple too many white wines if you know what I mean, Doc. Banged her head. You've probably seen the stitches?'

Ha ha bloody ha! Dad under pressure that's a good one.

'Yes, sorry, I didn't explain this very well. The fall, what can I say? Well, it sort of activated this behaviour, but the cause of her stress, that's what we're not sure of. It could be something trivial like a problem at work or a personal problem even? If you can think of anything in particular that could be bothering Christine it would be of a great help?'

I decided I liked this Doctor Atwood bloke. He was straight to the bloody point, a no nonsense type of guy, one of the boys unlike the two fucking fudge packers that had taken to twitching and tapping by the side of me.

'Tell him Dad. Tell him about you and him.'

Chapter Fourteen

Two days after our initial visit Mam's condition improved. Her behaviour calmed down dramatically although her depression worsened. Doctor A, sympathetically, said it was the stress of the situation. Dad and Mike stayed in the valley with Crazy Nan and Bamp even though I insisted they go back to Cardiff. Benders. I didn't want the fuckers about and as far as I could tell neither did Mam.

I stayed with Mam's Mam, Nanna and the old man. The old man is Nanna's partner Clive, he's a really tidy bloke and as soon as I dumped my bags in the spare room he handed me a can of Guinness. I appreciated the gesture and the way he tutted Nanna for shouting about giving me alcohol. I'd just about settled on the big leather sofa to watch the footy when Lisa, Mam's sister came in.

'Come on then boy.'

'What?' I wasn't giving her the sofa. She could piss right off. There was a perfectly good bloody arm chair across the mat.

'Get your kit on. We're off up the club.'

'You what?'

'There's a disco up the club dickhead. You're coming with me.'

'You want me to come with you?'

'Christ almighty. Get your clothes on kiddo you can get the first round in.'

It was seven twenty when we got to the club. There were only a couple of people sat round placidly sipping their club, priced beverages. Lisa waved and I nodded because; surprise, surprise of course we knew everyone there. DJ Bunny was at the bar as Lisa ordered two pints of Strongbow.

'Lisa baby, looking good as ever.'

'In your dreams, Sean. Can I get a straw, please?'

Bunny shot her a look of disgust than spun round to me.

'JJ ma man! How's Neil these days? Heard he got himself a boyfriend?' I couldn't tell if his tone was one of sarcasm, concern or even gloating. 'Nice little Italian so I'm told.' Imagine you're on a cliff top. The wind whistles through your ears, tingling into your brain. Your face is numb because it's fucking cold up there. Freezing in fact. The clouds swirl and amble through the sky. It's another day, another fucking day for them but for you, yes you, it's a moment. Alright it's a moment in a mere existence when you look at the big picture but nevertheless a moment.

This was a moment, a fucking horrible, horrible moment as flashing fucking images of my Dad, Mike, my mother's cut on her head, the quiet boy in my maths class who everyone suspects of being a poof, Lisa laughing, Meeky and the boys laughing but most of all this ugly fucking prick in front of me, laughing. DJ fucking Bunny.

'Alright Jon?' Lisa snapped me right back to the club, suddenly the music was audible and the clouds had gone. Bunny clicked his tongue and gave me two thumbs up as he walked back to his booth. Smirking.

'Jon!' my face must have said it all. If I'd had a mirror I'd bet myself a tenner that the vein in my head was throbbing.

'What did he say to you? Stupid Prick!'

'Nothing… Don' worry about it.'

We sat at the table and waited for Lisa's mates to turn up. The music was loud and the cider tasted good and thank

God it slipped down really easily. By my fifth pint Bunny's comment was just a hazy worry that seemed miles away from me and the club and the cider and I was beginning to enjoy myself. Lisa was leathered and her mates were all a good laugh. Mam crossed my mind a couple of times but Doctor Atwood had told me I couldn't do anything to help and to get on as normal, and I bet to everyone else in the club I probably personified normal! I mean what wasn't normal about this situation?

Well, that question was shortly answered for me when the boys turned up.

Chapter Fifteen

'Alright Meeky lad?" Meeky stared back without saying a word. Now, at this point I was pissed, but even minus several brain cells I realised something was wrong. You can just tell, cant you?

'Meek?'

'I need a word, Jon.'

I wobbly followed my friend to the car park.

'What's happening, Meek?'

Meeky looked strange. The only other time I'd seen him look like that before was … Oh no. The only other time I'd seen him look like that before was when he beat shit into Hwyel Morgan. Hwyel was shagging a bird Meeky was knocking about with at the time. Meeky had waited until after school then kicked the crap out of the poor sod.

'I think you know what's wrong, Jon.'

'Meek, I have no idea what I've done.'

Bang!

No explanation. Just a punch. I stumbled round the side of a Ford Fiesta, because fair play to the boy, he had one hell of a right hook.

It was only as my vision sort of resumed a normal position that I realised Meeky was not alone.

'Alright Jon? Heard you've been keeping a little secret from us haven't you?' Wedgy. God, this was going to hurt.

'You fucking Bent Bastard.' Bang. Nice one Wedge, don't think you quite broke my ribs mate.

Bang. Bang. Bang.

I was on the floor now. My head was scraping across the tarmac. My nose was bleeding and my body was taking an alarming amount of knocks. I recognised a couple of trainers, obviously fists were a little more tricky although I know Bunny jammed his ugly hand into my already smashed face at one point because I remembered his stupid bling bracelet. I know for sure it was Meeky vocally egging my so called friends on, his tone was crystal clear even with one ear nearly embedded into the car park. His anger was so strong, I hoped that they'd go so far, they'd kill me.

'Son of a fucking gay. Can you believe it boys? His Dad loves cock and that fuckers been in the same bastard showers as us.'

They proceeded to beat and bruise me for, what felt like a further three days, then left me battered and bleeding to fuck.

It wasn't long before some nosy fucker found me and rung an ambulance.

Course Pansy and his fucking lap dog turned up in A and E. As if things couldn't get bloody worse. My nose had been broken, my eyes blacked, my ribs cracked and my right hand snapped, and here he is acting all macho telling his prick of a puppy what he'd like to do to the bastards. What he'd like to do to them? He had no fucking idea it was because of him I was in this fucking mess. The twat.

'I can tell you now, you're pressing charges. The little fuckers are gonna' get what's coming to them, the shits. I'd like to see them have a go at you one on one, wouldn't stand a fucking chance I bet...'

'Dad.'

'Bullies, nothing but bloody bullies they are,'

'Dad, please.'

'And where's the police when you need them? Nowhere to be seen look,'

'For fuck's sake Dad. Stop it!' I started to kind of whimper which I'm quite embarrassed to admit to now. It wasn't a proper cry or a wine just kind of the noise a puppy makes when you kick it. I mean I'd even started to sound like a bender, I deserved the kicking I'd got.

'JJ, I know this is hard, mate but ...'

'You don't even know the meaning of the fucking word. It's because of you I'm in this fucking mess, why my mother's in a poxy nut house and why I fucking hate you, you prick you fucking prick.'

There it was, the anger that had been simmering away in the cooking pot of my anger zone. And guess what? There was more.

'I don't even know why you're fucking hanging about. Mam doesn't need you, I don't even wanna' look at you in fact, I wish you was fucking dead.' I sort of screamed then which made a couple of nurses, a security dude and Lisa run in. Exit my Dad.

I know, I know there were much better ways to handle the situation but seriously my face looked like I'd swapped it with that of an alien beings, my stomach was tight as fuck, I'm sure my hair was going grey but most of all I was in fucking pain. Proper mind numbing, angry, ugly, sad pain, so really my little outburst was a tiny miny part of what I was going through. And the worse thing was I knew there were no easy escape routes.

After cleaning my chops, putting a cast on my wrist, giving me instructions, painkillers and antibiotics the hospital let me go. I had an appointment with them in a couple of days but yes, I was free to go home, or face the music in my case. We managed to get Martin, the taxi man, to take us back to Nan's.

'Ey, alright ,boy? In the wars there, kid."'

'Tell me about it Martin.'

'Never mind tell you about it. What the fuck are we gonna tell Mam?' Lisa, now sober and tired, having had to have waited with me for the last four hours, knew she was about to experience something close to the Spanish inquisition crossed with a massive bollocking when we got back.

I pondered the possibilities. Alien abduction could be an easy explanation. I walked into the door. It was all the diet coke I'd consumed? I got mixed up in an army training exercise?

Or the truth. My Dad's gay, the boys found out and give me a hiding because well, they think I'm contaminated.

'Oh, boy bach! What on earth has happened to him? Lisa, I told you no alcohol.' Nanna had started to cry, shuffling me into the living room and turning the television off. Most normal people would be in bed this hour, whatever hour it was.

'It's not what it looks like,' I offered.

'What do you mean it's not what it bloody looks like? You come in half dead...'

'He's not half dead,' Lisa said.

'Oh for Christ-sake Lisa, how old are you? What the bloody hell happened to him?'

'I got beat up."

"Well, I can see that, why? Who by? What for?'

'Want a Guinness kid?' Clive was awkwardly shuffling around on the pink carpet.

'No he bloody doesn't. It's probably that shit that got him in this mess.'

'Actually it's Dad's fault.'

'You what? He did this to you? Ring the police, Clive.

'No, no, he didn't do this. It's because of him, the boys did this.' my face and body were throbbing and it felt like there were bricks resting on my forehead. It felt like question time in school; now I know how that copper felt on careers day.

'Oh good God.' Nanna was still bleating on. But I was too tired to listen, just watched her mouth twitch in panic, until I was ushered to bed.

As soon as the lights were off the pain started. Humiliation is not the word and awkwardly I was forced from the soft sheets of my bed to the toilet, where I was sick and sick and sick.

Chapter Sixteen

'I am not going.' and that was final. Why on Earth would I ever want to see anyone again? For a start my face didn't even look like mine, and to be honest having spent fifteen years with it, I kind of knew what it's supposed to look like.

'JJ, it's not that bad,' Nanna was doing her 'everything's OK' impression. 'I'm sure it'll all blow over.'

Huh! Blow over, blow over? How the hell was it meant to blow over? Well, maybe if there was a freak tornado through the valley, it would blow over but failing that I was screwed.

'Here. I've made you corned beef sandwiches and everything.'

'And how exactly am I supposed to eat them, Nanna? Unless you've forgotten my friends beat the shit into me last night. I have a broken jaw, a smashed up hand, broken ribs and my face is so swollen I'll be surprised if I find my bloody mouth.'

'Now there's no need for that sort of language boy. I know you feel terrible but I'm sure there are better ways of expressing it.'

Oh really you daft bat? Better ways of explaining that my Dad's marrying another bloke so therefore my friends,

37

the friends I'm supposed to be going on a rugby tour with this morning beat the shit into me last night. Yeah no problem cutting out the fucking swear words.

'Well I'm not going.'

'You can't avoid them forever, JJ.'

Well, as far as I was concerned I could. In fact, last night in A and E, whilst I waited to be stitched, bandaged and plastered I made a life plan. Quit School, quit rugby, live in Nanna's spare bedroom for the rest of my teenage years, then once old enough run away to the North Pole where no one would ever find me. Perfect!

'Well, considering all I've done is buy bloody raffle tickets off you all year round to fund this bloody trip, oh yes, and your mother borrowed the deposit off muggings here for you to go, I've decided your bloody well going. Now grab your bag. Clive's been in the car for over half hour whilst you've been feeling sorry for yourself.' with that, Nanna frog marched me through the front door, into her partner's car and down the club before I even had a chance to mention I hadn't packed clean pants.

Chapter Seventeen

The bus was due to pick us up at eleven from the club. But of course the bastard thing was late. So, by ten past twelve I'd had two cans of Strongbow off Wedgy's Dad, a million dirty looks from most of the squad and several attempts at conversation with Rassoul.

Rassoul is a small lad from Dubai, who's Dad owns a battery factory on the North industrial estate. He's usually on the bench, and can only play scrum half, and to be honest, he can hardly play that. He hates the game, poor sod, but his Dad forced him into playing in an attempt to get his boy to bond with the locals, the club let him play a few minutes for a hefty sponsorship from his old man. Promptly I've never really talked to him really. Meeky's old man had been caught stealing batteries for Digger Dave from the factory and been sacked. Being a mini version of his Dad, Meeky naturally, holds one hell of a grudge therefore the team hold a grudge.

Now at this point I really couldn't afford to be fussy with my choice of friends and if Rassoul wanted to team up with me I was grateful that I wouldn't be spending the three hour journey up to Blackpool talking to my reflection.

Of course, when the shed of a bus finally pulled into the car park and the bags had been loaded, boarding the damn thing was the next dilemma. Getting up the steps with a practically broken body as the boys pushed they're way to the back seats wasn't exactly pleasant. Then I had to face the embarrassment of sitting right at the front with the boys *straight* Dad's, committee men and coaches.

'You want a crusp?' Rassoul had mastered most words of the English language; it was just the pronunciation that was the problem.

'No thanks, mate.' as I once again contemplated my injuries I wondered what would sustain me for the duration of the weekend, cider and soup?

The journey was pretty uncomfortable, as predicted, and only a few snide remarks about gay's/ fudge packers/ pansies were slung down the bus towards me. Although me and Rassoul hardly communicated I was grateful the seat next to me was at least taken, and as we saw the 'Welcome to Blackpool' sign we agreed to share a room. As the rooms shared four we arranged to bunk with Geraint and Tubby, another two loners. Wow! Wasn't I a luck boy? Whatever.

The rooms were basic. That's all I can really say. There was nothing spectacular about the décor that's worth describing. The only redeeming feature was the Dinosaur duvet covers on the two, blue framed, metal bunk beds that took up most of the space in the room.

'I can't believe I'm here.' Geraint half snorted, half laughed. 'I'm mega excited, I can wank all day and all night without anyone calling up the stairs "Geraint, what are you doing to yourself?" I can't wait!' his face had gone pink, and I instantly hoped while he shook and giggled that I wasn't above or below him on the bunks.

'Wonk? It is what?' Jesus, I thought at this point, if I didn't kill myself, or the boys get hold of me again to kill me by the end of the weekend it would be a miracle.

After we'd dumped our stuff and shot gunned our bunks, we all met in the lobby of the, well I wouldn't call it a hotel because it was more like a hostel or a foreign prison of some sorts.

'Right boys, we got a game in the morning so I want you all in tip top condition. So, basically I don't care if you get arseholed tonight, but be bloody sober for kick off tomorrow. Right?' Wedgy's Dad gave the group a wink and a ripple of laughter went round the room. I was the only boy who wasn't smiling. This tour had been the topic of conversation all season, God, the things me and the boys had planned, and now here I was in Blackpool with a foreigner and two bloody wanking nerds. There was no way those geeks were going to even think about going in a pub, let alone try and get in a lap dancing bar. And, I bet trying to even pull a bird is going to be completely out of the question not to mention impossible. The three of them were ugly bastards.

'So, be careful lads, keep your mobiles on and we'll do likewise. You've all got our numbers if there's a problem. Have fun.'

With that a whoop of joy was screamed and the lobby type place was emptied via any possible exit. (Davy Williams's legs could be seen sliding through the dog flap. Yes our hostel/prison was dog friendly.) I thought about sneaking back upstairs to hide under the nearest T-rex but the thud of two heavy hands on my shoulders soon stopped me in my tracks.

'AAAAAAAAAAAARRRRRRRRRRRRRRR!'

'Sorry boy. Are you OK? I totally forgot about your injuries,' Wedgy's Dad, Adrian smiled nervously down on me.

'Yeah. I'm OK, I think.

'Wanna' come with us, kid? You're guaranteed a couple of beers if you're with us lot. You get one of those fake ID's of Digger Dave?' My gratitude at that moment for Adrian was so strong I could have easily balled my brains out there and then.

'Do you mind?'

'Course we don't. First round on you mind, Kid.' he winked and manoeuvred me to the door.

Chapter Eighteen

Now, I can tell you everything about the first pub we went in, for the simple fact, I was sober in the first pub. You could ask me any question about the place. Décor, prices, clientele, absolutely anything. The next pub, is another story. I have hazy details of several hen parties. A lady called Stacey who was a particular hen, whose hens were dressed, literally as hens. Before Blackpool I had never seen a chicken with actual breasts. What a crazy place.

'Alright Kid?' I tried to focus on Adrian who appeared to be rapidly shaking back and fore in front of my eyes.

'Erm, yeah. Tidy actually.' I had to shut my one eye to see him properly.

'I think 'Cheeky Chick Clare' has got a thing for you kid.' he nodded in the general direction of the hens.

'You wha'?' God, cider with men, real men made me confused.

'Think you've pulled mate.'

Pulled? Me pulled? Wow this trip was turning out to be absolutely brilliant. I mean, at first I'd had no friends and a mangled up body, and OK, my body was still bruised and bandaged but here I was getting leathered with my coaches in a pub where a girl was eyeing me up. Me, little Jon Jones from Ebbw Vale.

I was clearly aware at this point, that my cider visors were well and truly activated (actually that's a big fat lie, the beer goggles theory was an afterthought) but the hen Adrian pointed out didn't look to bad. I had a little problem checking her out because it's really difficult having to perv with only one eye, not to mention highly annoying.

Anyway, from what I could make out after several ciders mixed with quite a high dosage of painkillers, 'Cheeky Chick Clare,' (she had that on her t-shirt) had sort of red, long hair with a pleasant face, nothing remotely striking but nothing ugly or grotesque. She seemed to have a nice figure from what I could make out, although it's a tad awkward trying to work out anyone's figure when their covered in feathers.

'Go speak to her.' Dingo, the forwards coach said whilst unashamedly ogling 'Bride Bird,' 'She looks a bit older than you to, you like um' older son?'

Oh God! Oh God! Was that a trick question for; are you a bender like your old man? Shit, why hadn't that even crossed my mind? I had to think of a pretty un-insinuating reply.

'I like them any age Ding.' I smiled at him while he leered.

'Me too, me too.'

Myself and Dingo then spent a rather tedious half hour discussing, at length, the hen's breasts. Which would have been a perfectly normal, manly thing to do. However, a lesson I learnt on that tour is; cider makes people loud.

'Excuse me boys?' I raised my very heavy head and shut my bruised eye enabling me to just about make out the shape of an angry chicken. I smiled up at it and giggled at the hilariousness of a woman dressed as a chicken. The giggling turned into full blown laughter and soon Dingo had joined in.

'Think its funny do you? Talking about tits. Well how would you find a sexual harassment charge? Funny maybe?'

All I could piece together in my mind was; chicken, tits, sexual something and laugh. So, that's what I did. Helpless was probably the best way to describe me.

'You two are absolute pricks, you know that?'

God, the woman could bang out questions. I was vaguely aware that the rest of the coaches, including Adrian and the committee members were all cheering the chicken on, which of course made me laugh even more. I'd got to the point of very nearly pissing myself when something extraordinary happened.

'Take no notice of her, she's a proper feminist. Burning the bras and all. I'm Clare.'

The laughing stopped along with all rational brainpower.

'I'm, um, um...'

'Jon?' she had a really nice smile.

'Yeah. How'd you know?'

'It's on your shirt, pet.' she giggled a bit and sipped an odd colour drink from a glass shaped like a willy.

'So, you from Wales? Obviously a rugby tour, yeah?'

'Yeah. The annual one.' God, why did I sound like such a knob. I took a sip of my pint and missed my mouth. The cider ran all down my chin, soaking my shirt and my crotch. Cheeky Chick Clare then did something incredible. She grinned, licked my chin and rubbed my crotch. Where my willy was like. I couldn't believe it.

'You get those bruises from rugby? I love rugby. The men are so sexy.' Her face was right behind my ear.

How could I even contemplate speaking? My swollen jaw had dropped around about where my knob rests. She had a northern accent, and when her lips moved she had some sort of shiny gloss on it that reflected the light. She was definitely older than me but only by about two, possibly three years. I was in love.

43

'Yeah. Rugby.' I finally managed after I'd coughed, twitched and squeaked a bit.

'They look sore, but dead sexy. How old are you, pet?' now, Dingo had told me if anyone asked I was eighteen and a bit, but did he mean bar staff and stuff or everyone?

'I'm eighteen and a boat.' damn!

'Eighteen and a what?' she smiled and I felt my crotch area stir.

'Eighteen and five months, I think.' God! I can't remember why I looked at her chest area when I lied but boy, I wish I hadn't. She had enormous, pale, round breasts. They were the most spectacular thing I had seen. Even better than Blackpool tower. When she moved or giggled they bounced ever so slightly in the tight t-shirt.

'I'm seventeen. I like the older man,' she giggled, boobs bounced. 'Especially one who plays rugby.' she rubbed my arm and I flinched slightly.

'Sorry, my arm took a bit of a beating.'

'God, I love your accent. Which part of Wales are you from?' and the conversation went on like this for a couple of hours. She continued to touch me and flirt quite a bit. At one point I thought I was way out of my depth when she asked was I hard.

'Excuse me?' I spat. Some of my cider escaped from the side of my mouth and I hoped the 'excuse me?' came across as; 'I'm sorry I didn't hear what you said?' Not a; 'excuse me I'm a virgin.'

'You know. On the field, do you play a position where you have to...what's it called? *Scrum*! Do you have to scrum?'

It was around about nine o clock when the hens decided it was time for a club. Luckily the older of the chickens had teamed up with the coaches and we all arranged to move on to somewhere a bit livelier.

Chapter Nineteen

The Star Club, was somewhere underground. I remember having to walk down shit-loads of steps to get into the place. I had no problem with having to show Digger Dave's fake ID because The Star, wasn't the type of establishment that was fussy with clientele. I came to this conclusion, immediately because as soon as we got on to the dingy dance floor there were about thirty other boys with the same shirt on as me. Pale blue cotton shirts with Deri Cross Rugby Club Badges, so much for avoiding the boys.

To make your way to the bar you had to push and shove your way through the dancers. This chore wasn't made easier by the sporadically placed mirrors that decorated most of the club. Its quite difficult working out what's not a mirror especially if you've all got the same shirts on.

Clare stood close to me and I could feel her breath on the back of my neck. I couldn't tell you the point where we had started holding hands for the simple fact I can't remember I just remember thinking; holy shit.

'JJ, ya' gay. How are your ribs?' with that someone's fist smashed into the front of my torso. I don't know who it was but I immediately doubled over. The cider had eased my un-comfort since the afternoon; that punch was like a top up of pain, just a reminder that I had absolutely no friends and that I wasn't welcome.

'Jon, are you OK?' Clare was kneeled on the floor next to me. My eyes were watering from both the pain and the smoke that filled the stupid cave thing we were in. The music thumped through my bones, beads of sweat began seeping through my skin, I had to do something.

'Yeah. It's nothing. You want a drink?' now, I didn't know this girl very well but I could see the concern take over her expression.

'Do you think you should have another one?' she looked around. 'Or would you rather go home?'

'No, I'll have another drink.'

'Jon, I mean home with me?' she then leaned into me ear, 'To bed.' she ran her tongue down my jaw, to my mouth softly brushing my lips until she'd parted them and pushed her wet, soppy tongue down into my throat, waggling it against mine. The word wow whizzed through my brain down to my knob. When she stopped kissing me she rubbed the back of my neck. 'Come on lets go.'

Obviously logical, sober thoughts like, 'I need to tell someone where I'm going' and 'God, did the boys just seen me kissing a chicken; is that worse than another boy?' And, 'I don't have a condom', didn't cross my mind. The drunken, delirious with cider ones like, 'wow, I'm going home with a woman', 'wow, she has big, bouncy boobs' and 'wow, I'm about to loose my virginity', did.

Chapter Twenty

'Can I get a kebab?' wasn't really what I'd expected as we emerged from the club.

'Yeah course.' Clare bopped over the road to Blackpool's answer to Turkish cuisine. 'Randy's Kebabs' looked like environmental health's dream. Cartons and tipped food smeared nearly every tile and table, drunk's of both sexes were sprawled and placed in all corners. There was even one couple practically shagging on one of the plastic chairs.

'You want anything?' Clare asked.

'No tit.' I answered as a gang of four or five girls pressed their naked nipples up against the window.

'Come on, you'll need your stamina you know?' Clare winked at me and here are some of the thoughts that clogged my brain while she waited for a chicken shish; Holy shit! I'm about to have sex and OK she doesn't look as pretty in the harsh light of 'Randy's Kebabs' but she is still a girl, a woman even. I am a boy, a boy whose father is gay. What if I don't enjoy it? What if I can't come? Shit, what if tonight I find out I'm gay. Jesus, how the hell am I supposed to pleasure her? What was that fella doing to that bird on that porno we all watched in Meeky's a couple of years back? I know he called her a couple of names. Did he put his hand on her thing? I know he leant her over a car but unless Clare's hotel is somewhere like Disneyland, props are going to be limited.

'Ready?'

'Yeap.' I swallowed hard, my throat actually made a gulp sound.

Clare's hotel was called, The Platinum. And its name was nothing to go by, although it was like a palace compared to the shit-hole where we were staying. She was sharing the room with Sharon, she said, although Sharon had pulled at breakfast and was unlikely to be back until the bus picked them up on Sunday.

'She loves cock does Sharon.' Clare was sat on the windowsill wolfing her shish down.

'Make yourself comfy.' she gestured at the double bed.

I manoeuvred as carefully and quietly as I could but with broken ribs, a sling and a smashed hand, neither were possible. The bed was dead bouncy and squeaked as I wiggled and whimpered onto the middle. I sighed, half in pain, half scared down to my shaking bollocks.

I was staring at the ceiling waiting for the pain to ease, as I'd found it did when I stayed still for a bit, when the room went black and a sound that can only be described as some sort of dolphin mating call echoed around the pink wallpapered double, en-suite.

'What the ...' I never got to finish my question because the previously feathered cheeky chick Clare had been plucked and was apparently horny as she belly-flopped onto my broken ribs and sprained arm, kissing and licking my bruised face as she slithered up and down the bed, firstly undoing my zip, feeling my dick and licking my mouth all at the same time. Then she ripped my shirt apart, oohing and aahing as she kissed my stomach.

'Aaaaooooowww.' was all I managed. I remember thinking if sex is this painful no wonder my Dad's a bender.

She was groaning like the bird in Meeky's film had, so I thought perhaps it was a good time to slip in; 'Give it to me you dirty whore.' she stopped dead in her tracks and because it was pitch black I had no idea which direction her palm would be coming from but as I braced myself for the slap she put my tackle in her mouth. No warning just straight in between her lips. I felt her head bobbing up and down on top of me.

'Oh God!' I whispered, she replied with;

'Meow!' and a little giggle which if I'm truthful unnerved me a bit. Why was she making cat noises? 'You like?'

'Don't stop!' fair play her head started bobbing again and did for what felt like a very pleasurable few hours.

'My turn now, Welshy. I want some fun.' with that she had straddled me, screaming something I couldn't quite make out, although I definitely heard 'cowboy.' She bounced about on me and I could feel my pleasure rising to my stomach, my throat, my brain and my knob.

'Yee Ha!' She screamed as she flopped her breasts in my face, which would have been nice I imagine if I wasn't so claustrophobic. I mean, they were huge and when they covered both my nose and mouth I panicked slightly. Luckily it wasn't long after I stained the sheets.

'You are an eager cowboy ain't you, Welshy?' It was only after she turned the bedside lamp on, dismounted me and came back from the bathroom armed with tissue's and towels did I realise she was wearing a pink fluffy Stetson.

'Here you are, get clean sweetie.' she threw me a toilet roll which I used to wipe my old boy. She was still bollock naked and fair play to the girl she had a cracking figure.

'What you looking at?'

'Nothing. Sorry, I didn't mean to stare. Nice hat.'

'Yeah I know. Now piss off.'

'Sorry?'

'You heard. Piss off.'

'Why?'

'Because I'm only here another day and I need to shag at least another three blokes to win the game.'

'What game?' I was young and naked, slightly insecure and the girl I just lost my virginity to was banging on about some game and instructing me to leave the hotel room.

'The Bag As Many Shags game, idiot, now piss off, its still early I may get another one in tonight.'

I heaved myself up from the bed, covering my dick as I did, grabbing my clothes with my good hand and escaping to the bathroom to keep my remaining tiny bit of dignity in tact. When I came back out looking slightly ruffled, Clare looked like another girl. She had taken the hat off and brushed her long, red hair so that it looked perfect. She was wearing a very small silver top that made her boobs look massive and a very, very small black skirt that made her legs look longer than the lit up tower.

'I'll walk out with you, pet.' she'd also reverted to nice, friendly, slightly flirty Clare.

As we got to the lobby of the hotel, she spun round to face me.

'Cheers for that, babe. You were good,' she kissed me on the cheek, 'got me in double figures.' With that she shrugged her shoulders, grinned and departed back into the sleazy wilderness that is Blackpool on a Saturday night.

Chapter Twenty-One

Don't get me wrong I wasn't stupid enough to think the earth was going to move or fire works go off or anything like that, I'm no girl. What I hadn't expected was to get banged by a chicken, for a game and then get dumped immediately after. God, I'd been used! Me, a boy, used!

49

Wasn't I supposed to do the using? All I hoped was that the boys never got wind of the mess that was my virginity.

As I wandered back to the hotel/hostel to try and get back to the safe comfort off my bunk, I really hadn't banked on running into the boys. And when I did run into them, I suppose the situation wasn't helped by the fact my shirt had been ripped, I reeked of perfume, Clare's lip gloss was smeared all over my face and I was heading in the completely wrong direction to where we were staying.

'My Dad's gonna' murder you.' Wedgy was quite clearly pissed; I mean he was engaging in a conversation with me for a start.

'Why?' there were a million sets of evil eyes just staring at me. I decided to stare at the road beneath me. Where it had rained the tarmac glistened, reflecting the neon lights of hotel signs and fast food places. The air had a tang of cheapness about it as I inhaled what I believed to be my last breaths. I hoped my mother realised how much I loved her and I hoped my Dad would rot in hell for putting me through this, the bastard.

'Because you've been gone hours.' Wedgy hiccupped and I could hear Meeky talking into his phone, telling whoever was on the receiving end;

'We've found the prick. Yeah he's fine.'

'I wasn't that long, was I?'

'Only about *three* hours Dick Head,' Wow, shagging takes time.

Wedgy was steaming. His eyes were sparkly and he was swaying and smiling at me. 'So then?'

'So then, what?' I smiled back at him. I wasn't going to give too much away in case he was bluffing and about to kick shit in to me, *again*.

'Did you get your end away then?' He was really smiling then.

'I might have.'

'You did. You did. You did, didn't you?' Wedgy sort of bounced about and smacked my back. All the boys joined in, laughing and cheering and finally my shoulders lowered and my body relaxed.

'Jon?' the laughing stopped.

'You know you've shagged a chicken, don't you?' Meeky's tone was my shoulders cue to rise once again. 'So, not only is your old man a fucking gay,' he spat in my direction. 'But, you've shagged a dirty fucking chicken.'

. Silence. A horrible, tumbleweed silence. I looked at the faces of my so called friends and considered what fate they had in store for me this time. They'd broken my ribs, smashed my hand, and bruised my face, what was next? Rip my eyeballs out? Brain damage, a possible castration?

'Only joking JJ, well done my son.' Meeky tapped my back and pulled me into an awkward hug (a manly one mind,) 'I'm sorry, mate.' he said it quiet enough for only me to hear and who knows, maybe I wouldn't have been so touched if I wasn't pissed and hadn't just got laid, but I could have cried with gratitude. Thank God, I had got my friends back.

'Well done Jon knew you had it in you, mate.' Wedgy was still wobbly.

The patting on the back and manly cuddles continued for about half hour (five minutes sober time,) although it was only Meeky that apologised, I knew in their own way they felt bad about what had gone on though.

'Come on then, J lets get you back to Dingo, he wants all the sordid details. Come to think of it, so do I, mate?' Meeky laughed and directed me gently towards the hostel. 'Come on then?'

'What do you want to know?'

'What was her bucket like, boy?'

Chapter Twenty-Two

Before we went back to the hostel, Adrian had ordered us to the pub opposite to report in. As soon as I walked in, the bar started clucking at me.

'JJ, Adrian giggled. 'Come and sit by Uncle Ade and tell me all, boy. Get the lad a pint Dingo, I want details.'

'Get the lad a pint my arse the little shit can have a glass of Coke to sober him up. You've had me worried shitless. Was she worth it?'

'I'd laugh my knob off if you had bird flu, JJ.' Wedgy nearly pissed himself at his own joke.

Now, this was more like it. Back with my boys being treated like a bloke. As long as we never run into Clare again, not much could go wrong.

'Well,' I started. 'Where to begin?' and I relayed the happenings of my stolen virginity.

The next morning I woke up drunk. Rassoul was spitting at me in what I hoped to be his native language, or I had definitely had way too much the night before.

'Hold your horses, mate. I got no idea what you're on about.'

Tubby's round face turned a sort of mortification pink and Geraint couldn't look at me. Rassoul continued pacing round the small room, waving his arms and shrieking in his Superman pyjamas.

'What's he on about, lads?' Tubby simply pointed at Rassoul's bed. Being on top bunk and still extremely bruised I was forced to kind of grab and hang to see what the fuss was about.

Holy Shit.

No.

No, couldn't have been.

Rassoul had stopped dead in his tracks and his big brown eyes swelled like a flushed toilet, his bottom lip trembled and for some mad reason his right leg started to bounce up and down.

'Look. Look at what you're done.'

'Oh God.' Was all I could muster. Rassoul's dinosaurs were now covered in a green/ yellow substance. The room stunk of spew and piss and it wasn't until I readjusted my bottom half's position did I realise I had obviously been the creator of this God awful scent.

'He's been on the floor all night,' Tubby looked as embarrassed as I was beginning to feel, and as I quickly began to sober up, I can tell you. 'Well, none of us have slept to be honest. You came in pretty late, then this…' he gestured to my mess, then gave out a nervous sort of giggle.

'Boys, I …' then it started, a sickening pain in my stomach, a throbbing, uncomfortable twang in my lower abdomen. 'shit, shit, move,' now, just in case my life could have been made a tiny bit more difficult my ribs ceased up and my bones ached from my toes to my scull, Shit, how the hell had I got up on top bunk last night? How true it is about that stuff that you feel nothing whilst under the influence.

'Boys, quick!' I had no idea what I thought these Dickheads could do, they were like farts in a car for Christ sake. There was one last pain and a horrible (yet beautiful) sense of relief. Bugger.

'Um,' I had to think fast (which has never been a strong quality of mine) 'um, I think I've pissed myself.' As soon as the lie left my swollen lips I knew it had been a mistake.

'Oh! Again, again!' Rassoul covered his face. 'My poor bed!' he whimpered. Everyone became incredibly silent.

Oh shit! How was I supposed to explain this. I knew from the moment the pain in my stomach squeezed itself to my lower body that I had indeed, shit my boxers.

I made an attempt to shuffle closer to the edge of the bed, Christ I'd started to buzz and the drop to the floor looked worse than the Big bloody Dipper. There was no way out of this, unless I sat in my own shit and filth until everyone left to play rugby? No, it was no use the lads would pick up the stench from here, (the even worse stench I might add, cause it was bound to get worse that, that I'd already created.) pretty damn quick.

53

Right. I'll try the angry approach, which always seemed to work for Mam.

'Oh, for fucks sake.' I made a big gesture of staring at my pants, breathing heavily through both of my nostrils, then for added drama I rubbed my eye's (which really hurt my head and made me wince) In the most dignified manner possible, I manoeuvred my whole body so that I was able to lower my sore self onto the highly unstable ladder being careful to drag the itchy blankets with me. (Dinosaurs were a useful alibi I discovered.)

'I've shit myself! As if things couldn't get any bloody worse, I've crapped my bastard pants.'

Geraint and Tubby just blatantly stared. Rassoul or Prince Rassoul as I'd that minute labelled him began sobbing. Big, breathless sobs that any diva would be immensely proud of. In later years I will probably describe this moment as traumatising.

'Stop fucking staring at me, I've shit myself.' Dumb and dumber averted their eyes and Prince simply bolted to the nearest exit which unfortunately happened to be the fire escape.

My cheeks on both my arse and my face burned like the flames of hell as I shuffled, limped, shuffled, limped to the communal pans, with itchy sheets and dinosaur duvets wrapped round me like a novelty bloody toga.

The walk down the corridor to the communal shower room made me think of how death row inmates must feel. Every door I passed felt like a small conquest, the closer I got to the 'wash room' the faster I dragged myself over the mankey green carpet that the hostel/ hotel/ prison must have got at knock off price as it seemed to be in every bloody room.

'What you doing, JJ butty?' oh, for fucks sake. Someone upstairs was really bastard frowning upon me (or giggling, whichever way you want to look at it.) My palms and upper lip began collecting small beads of sweat. I could feel my blood pressure pumping up several notches. Do I turn? Do I carry on? Or do I simply collapse on the floor and pretend to be dead?

'Um,' was all I mustered.

'You alright or what?'

'Um, not really…no.' I still hadn't turned round so I had no idea who was interrogating me although I could feel their eyes burning into my seeping arse.

'Anything I can help with?'

'No ta, butty.'

'OK, see you in a bit.' I heard, whosever door shut and relief clouded my entire body as I locked the shower cubicle behind me.

After compulsively scrubbing the dinosaurs until they resembled pale looking dog things and scrubbing my aching body until it not only ached but bloody stung too. I shimmied back to my room where I stuffed the remaining soiled sheets from both my bed and Rassoul's, into carrier bags, (I'd chuck them after, I thought) I sprayed most of the beds, walls, carpet and generally anything that may smell with my Christmas Lynx set that I'd saved especially for tour.

I still felt like complete shit (excuse the pun) but I spiked my hair, chucked my joggers on and limped down to the lounge to meet everyone.

The boys took over the communal lounge area of the hotel. Everyone was remotely subdued in their pre game, post Friday night alcohol intake, which was generally expected on tour. Wedgy was playing on the gambling machine, Meeky was sprawled over two paisley sofas plugged into his I-pod and the coaches/ dads poured over the team sheets and fresh pints on too small tables. There was no sign of Rassoul, Geraint or Tubby which was another relief, hopefully my little episode would go

reasonably unnoticed, just like my arrival into the lounge
…

'Here he is!' it was then a verse of 'chick, chick, chick, chick chicken, lay a little egg for me.' Chorused around the room. My cheeks coloured.

'Alright, alright. Aren't we the effin' comedians.' the boys laughed and for the first time in weeks I felt normal, back in the game, as those Yank rappers say.

'And …' Wedgy screamed. 'First boy on tour to shit himself.' Oh shit.

'You know what that means lads.' Meeky looked unfazed and unsmiling. Oh shit. I hope the association between, shitting myself and having a loose arse hole and having a gay father which would in turn make me a raving bender, wasn't going through everyone's mind like it was mine. 'It can only mean …' holy shit, someone tell my Mam I loved her, because I was surely about to meet my fate.. 'Deeees –gust-ting!!' the boys echoed the word until the whole room was chanting it.

'Deeees-gus-ting! Deeees-gus-ting! Deeees-gus-ting!' all the boys were pointing at me.

'Shame on you.' Wedgy grabbed my shoulder and handed me a can of Carling. Now I was confused.

'Go on then,' he beamed. 'You didn't think you'd get away with it, did you?'

The chant changed.

'Down it! Down it! Down it!'

Thank God.

Chapter Twenty-Three

Obviously I couldn't play rugby. Not because I'd downed seven cans of Carling before vigorously throwing up in the nearest plant pot (which was thankfully home to a fake tree thingy.) and it wasn't because I had been violated by a chicken the night before, shit myself or got seriously hammered on the golden mile, it was because of the little kicking the boys had given me a few days previous, but hey what's a couple of broken ribs between friends?

I'd like to say we annihilated the opposition but I'd be blatantly lying. We did rattle them like, but it wasn't through our rugby skills, it was the fourteen and a half greasy cooked breakfasts that the ref had to stop the game for, so they could be brought back up on the sidelines ten minutes into the first half. Wedgy only brought half of his food up declaring he'd swallowed the rest, as he didn't want to waste it.

Sloppy from the night before our boys let the big Blackpool buggers run away with a 40- 6 lead. And we only got two penalties cause Meeky pleaded then accused the, slightly intimidated referee, of being racist.

'Its just cause we're Welsh.' He'd exploded.

There were several scuffles which is nothing new with us lot. Wedgy broke his finger and Rassoul (who I was starting to really sympathise with) got a black eye, and the poor sod wasn't even playing, just happened to be in the wrong place (the sidelines) at the wrong time.

Meeky managed to bully his way to man of the match. I think it's because he also threatened the ancient ref to blow the whistle about five minutes before the game was due to end. To be honest, the ref was about seventy five and looked like he was due to croak it a mere three minutes before the game was due to start!

We were fed sausage, beans and chips in the clubhouse after the game with about four hundred pieces of bread and butter, washed down with a couple of drinking games.

I was getting right into the tour spirit and I have to admit I was starting to really get a grip on the old alcohol intake. It wasn't until the games had calmed down and everybody grouped off in selective huddles that I noticed Rassoul in the corner of the club, on his own sipping cider through a pink straw.

'Are we ready to hit the town then, boys?' Meeky interrupted my slurred thoughts as everyone stood, downed and made their way to the exit. Rassoul seemed to loiter behind everyone. The invisible prince was a phrase that sprung to mind.

'Rass?' he looked scared like I was about to projectile vomit all over the poor bugger. 'Rass, please. Look buddy I'm really sorry about last night. I wouldn't have done it on purpose.'

'My bed!'

'I know, mate. It was cause I was drunk, I didn't … I didn't know what I was doing.'

Rassoul sighed and put his head down. 'It's OK, it is.' he sucked his lips into a bit of a smile.

'Thanks Rass. Are you coming out?'

'No. no. no' he looked slightly embarrassed.

'Come on butt, I'm not taking no for an answer.' it was the second time in a couple of hour's diva Rassoul's eyes filled up but it was for different reasons, I hope.

We'd all planned to meet back in the Sickening Green lounge at six, and after spending the best part of forty-five minutes on Rassoul's outfit, I have to admit the boy looked pretty damn dapper. Geraint and Tubby could take care of themselves but I felt it was my duty to take Rassoul under my wing. I'd lent him one of my French Connection t shirts and I'd re-adjusted his jeans (after much protest, mind.) so they now sat lower than his belly button. I'd also really spiked his hair so it wasn't fluffy and flat – Now he could actually pass as teenage boy, not a poor bloody Egyptian beggar child thing. God, you'd never think his old man had money.

'I look good, yeah?' now I know how being a parent must feel. Seriously I could feel my heart swelling with pride as I looked at my little protégée.

'You'll do, butty.' I managed, and I swear to the trained ear I sounded choked. "Come on lets get going."

'What the fuck?' Meeky looked mad. 'What's he doing with you?' the room went quiet.

'He's coming out with me,' then what I can only describe as some sort of wave of bravery hit me smack in the guts. 'Is that going to be a problem?' I swear to God I could see tumble weed rolling round the room.

'If problem, I will stay here.' Rassoul flapped and for the first time EVER I thought shit, I couldn't actually give a flying fuck what anyone thought.

'You're coming Rass, even if it's just you and me.'

'You're all right boys, if Mr Meek gotta problem, yous twos can come out with us.' Thank the lord for Adrian! I mean, the first time I'd gone out with these fellas I'd lost my virginity, perhaps we went out with them on a Saturday night I could get Rassoul's virginity taken care of and maybe I'd even end up pulling something marginally smarter than a bloody chicken?

'Actually I'd rather go out with you lot too.' Wedgy stood behind me putting his big paws on both my shoulders. A bit like an over protective body guard, and if you could personify (latest word I'd learnt) my gratitude it would have surely been the size of the worlds biggest elephant.

Then the weirdest thing happened, an echo's of 'me toos' pounded off the walls and before I knew it most of the boys were lined up behind me.

'Well, Meek. You coming out with us, or what?' I didn't think Adrian taunting Meeky was a very wise idea myself but I was hoping that being an adult he had years and knowledge and a bit guts too, on his side. Meeky's face was dead pan and I couldn't help admire his stance, his black Armani shirt and stonewashed jeans. All in all, the boy was a good package. A couple of minutes ago his presence in the room would have frightened me shitless, but now with my small army behind me he resembled a teenage boy who had been top dog for far too long.

'What we waiting for then? Let's go.' Meeky answered smiling as if nothing had happened, but I'd felt the balance shift.

'Come on then. Let's see what Blackpool's made of.' and everyone piled out through the lobby.

'JJ, hold it.' and here comes the punches no doubt, I screwed my face up ready for the initial smack.   'Look butty...I'm sorry, sorry about everything.' Meeky looked young and strangely vulnerable, I want to say that without sounding like a complete pansy, by the way.

'It's alright.'

'We're OK, yeah?'

'Yeah, butty, we're OK.'

And that was that. We went on to hit Blackpool with a vengeance, as rugby tours do, and to be honest I have very little recollection of that Saturday night.

Boarding the bus Sunday morning after another cooked breakfast the mood was tipsy, that's the only way I can describe it. Apparently, we got back to the prison block (as the hotel had now been renamed) at four thirty. Obviously, not quite drunk enough we had decided to demolish several bottles of Tequila, using apples and sugar from the 'breakfast room' as salt and lemon substitutes.

The bus had a lingering smell of stale beer and fart (caused by the stale beer, no doubt) I sat next to Rassoul who was suffering beyond belief. Last night had probably been the first time he'd ever been properly introduced to Alcohol, I'm sure they don't really drink where he's from. I think they may even get put in jail for it or something, or their hands cut off? Anyway, we hadn't long set off on the windy road to Wales when the crates were opened and the songs started as if we were just leaving for tour not returning. My bruises had started to go a shade of yellow/green (a bit like the prison block lounge) and my body only ached slightly when I moved.

I couldn't believe the whole thing was really over, all that planning and excitement to me almost dropping out, was over, dunzo for another year. And then the panic set in. A horrible, niggling worry creeping through my body at the prospect of returning home. I'd only given my Nan a quick ring when I'd arrived in Blackpool to let her know I was still alive and still feeling shite. So really, I'd had pretty much no contact with the green, green grass of home for almost three days, in which time anything could have happened with a family like mine.

Was Mam still nuts and Dad still gay? Time would only tell, I suppose. It wouldn't surprise me if I got home to find a Russian circus renting out my bedroom or even a big bloody hole where 'home sweet home' once was, only diggers and big yellow machinery left as clues to my old life?

'JJ. ARE. YOU. HOME. JJ?'

'Sorry Rass, I was miles away there.'

'Yes. I am aware. I was just wondering why you scratch so much?' Rassoul nodded his head and gestured to the general direction of my old boy, where strangely my right hand (I was very nearly ambidextrous) was engrossed in vigorously rubbing the whole surface area of JJ junior and for some reason flashes of chickens flashed through my conscience.

'Oh no.' groan!

Chapter Twenty-Four

A couple of days after I got back from Blackpool a sort of normal regime began. Well, when I say normal, what I mean is Mam was released (Is that the correct terminology for people suffering with a mental condition? Released?) From the hospital with shit loads of medication and even more weird habits. I continued to live with Nan whilst Mam got to terms with her illness apparently, Doctor Atwood told me, Mam was Bi-polar which basically meant sometimes she would be crazy-happy and other times she'd be crazy-sad so really, she'd pretty much be crazy all the time.

'The drugs will stabilize her.' Doc told me one day when I went round to our house. They were having coffee, which I thought to be a bit over professional but if he was making her better I couldn't really argue with the situation.

Anyway, over the next couple of weeks I gradually got used to her behaviour. Like when she was up, as in happy, the way she would compulsively clean the house, then blatantly piss herself in the kitchen declaring that she was; 'far too busy' to stop and use the toilet. And, when she was down, as in sad, how she would refuse to get out of bed, refuse to change her clothes, refuse to wash and even eat. Slowly I followed the mood patterns and learnt how to behave around her depending on whether she was Mam Up or Mam Down, that was.

One day I went round for my dinner and I couldn't get the front door to budge. After ringing the door bell several times, checked the bottom windows and started to think the worst (slit wrists, blue lights, a pink bedroom round Dad's for my remaining childhood) I could hear muffled tones of a Freddy Mercury song.

'Mam, you alright? It's JJ.' I assumed she'd lost the plot when she budged the door open wearing massive ear phones and bright pink lipstick.

'Sorry babe, didn't hear you. Doctor Atwood bought me an I-pod but I couldn't get on with those tiny ear things so I dug these out the attic. You OK baby?' she gave the door one last tug and disappeared into a mound of colours.

'Sorry babe.' she recovered herself off a pile of cushions. 'There's just so many.'

It was only when I got passed the welcome mat did I realise that Mam was on an Up Day.

'I made these. Been up all night I have.' she gestured to about four hundred Christmas cushions of various shapes and sizes.

'Mam, it's only June?'

'I know that silly.' so I just shut up.

It wasn't long after this episode when I bravely decided to move back home. I mean, half the time she was alright and at least I could keep a close eye on her if I lived there, even if she was a bit embarrassing. I thought, anything had to be better than Nan's constant supply of sandwiches until Mam started feeding me Alpha bites, spelling out mad phrases for tea like; '*I cant eat more than ten biscuits in one go*' and '*I don't like peas they are too green*' which as you can imagine, are a hell of a lot of Alpha bites on one plate. But, in all honesty it was all quite amusing. Far more fun than when she was suicidal over Dickhead leaving her. Talking about Dickhead, I hadn't heard or seen the shit since Mam had been admitted, which suited me down to the ground.

In fact, I was just getting used to a one parent set up (pretending I didn't or had never had a father) even if I was playing the role of parent eighty percent of the time, when HE turned up.

I had only popped to the Post Office one morning. The bastard must have been stalking outside, waiting to pounce on vulnerable prey, because when I got back there the twat was, drinking coffee and giggling round the breakfast bar with Mam. Now in a parallel universe this would be a very normal scene from a very normal terraced house, but considering the wanker had run off with a girl and was now marrying a boy, leaving my Mam to go absolutely bonkers, it was all a bit un-nerving.

Mam was painting her finger nails a sparkly purple shade and in mid flow explaining the rules and regimes of the mental institute when I made my presence clear with a staged cough that even the Shakespeare thespian company would have been immensely proud of.

What struck me as super strange was how old Dad had come to look. You'd think shagging a boy barley out of adolescence would do wonders for his appearance. Instead he looked weathered, drained. Even the bling earring had become dull, not so much of a spectacle, which I was pretty grateful for because hopefully it was less noticeable to the naive eye.

'What's up, J?' what's up, J? That's all I got? The bloke had practically ruined my life, nearly got me killed and he wants to know what's fucking up? Prick. I could feel the muscles in my face start to twitch.

'What are you doing here?' Mrs Lewis my old (as in previous) primary school teacher(although she was old) had once written on my annual report; 'Jonathan is a pupil who does not beat around the bush' it had come from an argument I'd had with the dithery old bat during a history lesson. I was adamant that during her era the world, as a whole, was in black and white not just the photographs. She blew it all out of proportion telling me it was rude to call people old, so I retaliated with the argument that she couldn't help being old! The whole thing ended up with me standing outside the classroom for a vast amount of that Tuesday afternoon.

'I didn't think you'd be pleased to see me.' was this guy for real? What the hell did he want? For me to embrace him, tell him secretly I'd been really pleased he'd come out and got engaged to a camp kid? For Christ Sake.

'I've come to see how your Mam's getting on. Well, to see how both of you are?'

'We're great. Never better. That OK for you? Thanks for coming.'

'J. Don't be rude, babe. It's nice to see your father.' Mam was shaking and her voice was quivery. God, I really did despise this bloke. My skin tingled as the atmosphere in the room got heavier. I wanted to lash out, to smash plates, throw everything, just get rid of this pent up anger he was creating but I knew I had to hold it together for Mam's sake. I bit my lip really hard in hope that the pain would distract me. The second my salty blood hit my tongue I felt my adrenalin prickle my eyes. Teasing my eyeballs into ripping my defence down and putting my emotions right out there, a big piece de resistance, on my bloody face.

'It's OK. He has every right to be angry.' someone applause the stupid fucker.

'You're still his father. He needs to remember that.'

'You think I've forgotten? You think the fact has slipped my mind? Christ you
really are mental.'

'That's enough.' Dickhead raised his voice. Mam had started to whine and I'm sure my nostrils couldn't expand anymore with all the air I was sucking through them.

'God, I'm sorry about all this J, but your 'gonna have to start accepting this situation.'

'Accept what? That you're gay and she's nuts because you're gay?'

'I. AM. NOT. NUTS!' Mam got off her stool, took her top off and started singing a ballad from Disney's Little Mermaid. Dad stood in wonder and I put my head in my hands.

It took us three renditions of the song before we could coax Mam into taking a sedative and put her to bed.

'How often does she do that?' Knob features had asked as I started cleaning the kitchen up. I wasn't doing it to be helpful or even as a distraction task to take my mind off Mam's outburst. I was just hoping if I looked busy enough he'd piss off.

'What do you mean, how often?'

'Well,' he made a nervous laugh sound. 'How often does she do mad things like that?'

'Try everyday, Dad, although I haven't heard that particular song before. She's ill!' I did a quick brain scan of my childhood and I can't ever remember him ever being that thick when I was growing up.

'I thought she was better, though. I mean the tablets?'

'They only stabilize her. It's not something that can be cured, it'll always be there.'

'Shit.' Dad rubbed his eyes and if I wasn't being too angry I may have felt a tad sorry for him at this point.

'Is there anything I can do?'

'Ha! I think you've done enough. Now, if you don't mind I have to get ready for training.'

'Sure. Do want a lift?' how's about NO you twat.

'No thanks.' and with that he left.

Chapter Twenty-Five

I was a bit dubious leaving Mam sprawled across the double divan whilst I meandered towards training, but Doctor Atwood re-assured me she'd be flat out until tomorrow some time. In fact, old Doctor A had been incredibly helpful since Mam had been home. Popping round with self help books, lotions and potions, several contact numbers on, what looked like, a personal business card and even some sort of casserole his mother had knocked up for us. If I wasn't so wrapped up in getting my life back into order, I'd have thought something fishy was going on.

Anyway, to justify buggering off to throw a ball round a pitch for the best part of an evening leaving crazy mother fucker drugged up and head down I kept picturing his face! I mean, the cheek, what the fuck was he doing coming round to our house? The house he left to shack up with a fella? (OK, not technically true, he'd left cause things weren't working out, but still...) I was just picturing the idiot having stones and various *large* objects being thrown at him when an old (and I mean, old) brown car pulled up, slightly fast besides the pavement.

'Alright kid?' how come Davy from next door always turns up when I really didn't need him to?

'Alright Davy? What's this?' I think the car was a Lade estate – although don't quote me on it, it was probably older than Steve the Barber.

'Well, funny story, J. I found it.' oh hell! How could someone have simply found an old estate car? I mean, we're hardly talking a fifty pence piece find are we?

'How'd you get it started, Buddy?' I peered to the dash area expecting to see wires and what not (There have always been rumours round the valley that Davy's sperm donor had been Digger Dave – perhaps hot wiring tactics were genetic?) instead, a key ring with what looked like a pink fluffy owl of some sort dangled from a key that was firmly in the ignition. Davy tutted and gave me an 'Ah bless he's simple' look.

'I just turned the key J, you need a lift?'

'Where exactly did you find it?'

'That's the funny bit Sonny Jim, or Sonny JJ,' he laughed at his own humour. I did a quick scan of the car/hearse/whatever and alarm bells started ringing in my already puzzled head, as I registered several full Tesco carrier bags, a duffle coat and yes, a Yorkshire Terrier on the back seat.

'It was outside the Post Office.' it was at that moment a cop car swung round the corner, straight past Davy, towards the Post Office flashing lights and all.

'Mega, wonder what that's about? Wanna' come find out?'

'Nah, you're alright Dave. I'm off training.'

'Tidy. See you after.' he than manoeuvred a nine point turn towards the Post Office. Oh heck.

For pre season training, the turn out was poor. There were only eight or nine boys stretching on the astro-turf, an abysmal number by normal standards. So, to say the atmosphere was slightly tense would be a severe understatement.

'Are we gonna bother then? Cause there's a double episode of Emmerdale on.' I've never understood why Wedgy's played for so long. He is one incredibly lazy shit.

'We're training!' Adrian's voice was a bit scary.

'Alright. Alright. Mam's taping it for me anyway.' he spoke quietly. Tonight Adrian obviously meant business if Wedgy backed down so quickly. Usually a substantial amount of banter would take place resulting in a play fight or so on.

'Get changed if you need to, if you don't start lapping the pitch.' Adrian rubbed his eyes and I immediately regretted coming, and after what felt like a full lap of the equator, a hell of a lot of mindless passing and some very hard tackles, I'd nearly decided to give the bloody sport up completely.

'Right boys, see you next week, and get the word about, I want more of you here next week.'

As we all worked towards the changing room we exchanged general miseries about training, the prospect of going back to school and the season ahead. And everything felt back to normal. OK, there was an awkward moment when Wedgy called Lee Davies, our proper scrum half, a faggot but in the end we all laughed it off.

Then something I can only describe as DREADFUL happened. Now I'll admit, the signs had been there since the return journey from Blackpool, and like I'd been doing since Dad's big news (Diversion tactics Doctor Atwood, later labelled it) I'd avoided thinking about the problem. And like most things you avoid the problem only ends up getting worse and worse, bigger and bigger, until its not only out of your hands but colossal.

Being late august it was hot. A typical valley summer as it goes and seeing as Adrian had just done his Hitler impression and just run us bloody ragged, we were all boiling so a shower was pretty essential.

Now, I'd just like to add at this point I really had lost all faith in higher poxy powers because if someone/thing is up there controlling the comings and goings in my life – they must fucking hate me!

I'd just lathered my head with Meeky's Head and Shoulders, spun round so the trickle of tepid water from our state of the art power showers (not) didn't go in my eyes when I heard;

'What the fuck, J?' if I hadn't been so relaxed I'd have picked up on the sort of stunned silence.

'Oh, it's where my ribs got busted. Looks odd 'don it?' it was only when I looked south did I realise the question hadn't been directed at my out of proportion ribs but my knob.

'What is it?' the boys had assembled in a small cluster directly in front of my dignity.

'Look's… look's painful buddy.'

My knob had only gone and got incredibly mankey. To be honest, I don't really want to give a poetic description of what appeared to be growing on my faithful steed. I'd known from the second Rassoul had pointed out my mindless scratching on our way home that something wasn't quite right but I'd found shit loads of plausible excuses to why old JJ junior wasn't feeling too marvellous; Numero uno – he was tired from tour. I mean, he'd had hell of a lot of action.

Two – didn't an immense amount of alcohol induce weird goings on in that area? And finally, Prison block A hadn't really been up to much, hygienically speaking.

So, it had been of no surprise really that my nether regions hadn't felt remotely normal since tour, but like most things, after a while you just sort of get used to it.

'Do you think it's contagious?' the boys took approximately two steps back. 'It looks a bit alien.' Faggot or no faggot Lee Davies was in for a hiding.

'It's um … a new washing powder.' why lie? I should have simply gone down the route of surprised/shocked. 'Yeah, It flared up last night, mad or what?' I let out a sort of strange giggle. If I didn't get out of the shower soon my whole body would shrivel up, and wouldn't that look bloody good on top of a gunky knob?

'I'm sure it's nothing to worry about.' I offered. God, why were they all staring like I had nine heads. Well, I suppose I did really.

'Um… J, I don't mean to be rude, but it looks like genital warts buddy. My brother went to Magaluf last year. Shag-a-luf he called it. Anyway, he came back with it. My old gal took him to A and E and everything cause she assumed he'd picked some scary disease up – you know, being abroad and all. Turned out he'd put it about quite a bit out there and caught warts. Mam went mad.' (I used to be in total ore of Meeky's older brother, Craig. He was a better looking version of Meeky and mega popular. Today I hated the prick.)

The idea had flicked through my poor conscience that I could have caught an STI, but to be honest it really had flicked in one brain cell and straight into my 'think about later' corner and I'd thought/hoped it would just clear itself up.

'I bet it was that chicken bird, JJ.' Wedgy's tone was sympathetic but his look was one of incredible amusement and as I scanned the boys who were all suitably towelled up (unlike myself) and lo and behold, they all wore matching expressions.

'What shall I do?'

'Doctors buddy. You got bird flu.' I don't know who said it, but it tickled me beyond belief and before I could register the seriousness of an STI, me and all the boys burst out laughing.

Chapter Twenty-Six

After I'd finally finished showering and got dressed, I was last in the changing rooms. Getting changed on my own meant I had time to contemplate my un well willy. God, why had I been so bloody stupid? I mean, that chicken

70

could be pregnant with my kid, or should I say chick? What a head fuck!

As I stuffed my crap in my kit bag, (good thing about Mam being 'not so good' as we'd labelled it, was that she didn't give a shit about washing now or whether clothes were folded or not) I rehearsed in my head what I'd tell the doctor, should I mention Dad is gay? God, what if I was diseased cause he's shagging men? Could I have caught something off him? God, I hope I didn't get the woman one. Mind, perhaps she'd be more sympathetic. Oh hell, how'd I get into this mess? My thoughts started drifting to the horrible stench of sweat and feet that made the changing rooms ever so pleasant to be in, when the door went and in Steve the Barber came. Thank god, my friend Steve. I'm sure the bloke was destined to turn up in my life when I really needed a rational brain.

'JJ butty, you OK?'

'Not really.'

'Um…is this to do with…?' he gestured to my groin. 'I just saw Meeky.'

'Oh God.' I forgot this type of news is hot gossip round the valley. 'Can my life get any worse Steve?' Steve sort of howled which made a huge show of his toothless gums.

'Course it can Boyo. These are little blips. You're growing up.'

'Blips? More like waves you mean.'

'You gotta be strong Kid. If not for ewe, for your Mammy and believe it or not your Dad.' I started to shake my very, very full head. 'Don't be forgetting he's human to, fella.'

Human? Course the twat's human, human and a bender. God, what did people take me for?

'How's things with you and him anyway?'

'Well, he was just in the house. I was civil.'

'Good boy. This'll get easier, Kid. I'm not saying you'll ever get used to him and … him, but it'll get easier.'

'Ha!'

'JJ…' he ruffled my hair. If anyone else had even touched me during this conversation I would have gone absolutely ape shit, but there was something about Steve's presence that soothed the atmosphere, made me feel safe, as if everything really wasn't that bad. '…have I ever let you down before?'

'No Steve. No you ain't.'

'Well then. Now piss off I gotta clean this place, poxy rotas.' I picked up myself ready to leave when …

'One more thing J. Get your self checked out tomorrow will you?'

'I will Steve.'

There was a small silver envelope on the breakfast bar when I got home. It was addressed to me. Well, the name written in very curvy handwriting was: Mr Jonathan Jones. I didn't recognise the scrawl but I had an odd feeling in the pit of my stomach. Mam was still out cold upstairs so the only person who'd had access to the kitchen had been my so called father. The sneaky bastard must have left it there as we were leaving.

When I moved it there was an identical envelope underneath it was addressed to Mam. Bollocks! Were they invites for the wedding, or with a bit of luck, copies of his will? My heart started pumping and sweat started bubbling on my top lip. Shit, he made me angry. What was he playing at? I mean he'd already destroyed Mam by coming out did he want her to fucking top herself or what? Images of gay boy Mike in a white dress and veil flashed through my mind and the drums in my temples started thumping and my nostrils flared like Black fucking Beauty's. Shit, those bastards had some nerve.

I was in two minds to just rip the invites up, but once again curiosity got the better of me. I sat myself down on the highly uncomfortable breakfast bar stools and slowly (with shaking and sweating hands) opened the envelope addressed to me. Perhaps they were cards saying sorry or letters saying they'd (as in him and bender boy) decided to move to Hawaii or something great like that? Whatever shit was in this letter/card/invite I was glad I was alone to asses the content – if it was too rough for Mam, I could hide them until she was feeling at least 99% OK.

I'm still not sure whether what I discovered was worse than what I'd imagined or sort of a relief. The small, highly camp, pink card invited Mr Jonathan Jones to a 'stag party.' Not a stag 'do' or a stag 'night' but a fucking stag 'party.' For fucks sake! It was to be in the rugby club, (the rugby club! Oh yeah I can see that place camping it up!) the Saturday before I went back to school.

Well, like hell would I be going to that for Christ sake. And why was Mam invited? Surely it's a bloke thing? Mind, saying that, surely it's a normal wedding thing. Was Dad the stag and Mike the hen, or the other way round? Or were they hosting a joint one? Oh lord why me? Why, out of all the possible people in Wales, the World even, why did my Dad have to be bastard gay? I was contemplating how shit my life had become over the last couple of months when a thought struck me smack in the realisation zone of my head.

If Pinky and Perky were having their 'party' in the club did this mean they were living in the valley? Please God say they hadn't set up pre marital bliss in the valley. The valley where if you had a new hairstyle or a new look you'd get the shit kicked out of you.' What would everyone make of two fellas living together not just sharing the rent but sharing toothpaste and bottles of wine and bloody bodily fluids. Holy shit they'd be hung, drawn and quartered. Not that I cared of course I just didn't want to be associated with the fuckers.

I was just wondering how, along with a nose job, a new writing hand and possibly a name change, would completely rid me of the twat when the phone started ringing.

'Helllooo JJ.' Oh no! It was Julie from next door. Why did she always ring instead of just popping round and why was she using a Scottish accent?

'Hi Julie.'

'Babes, any chance you could pop over? I need your help with something.'

'OK, be there now.'

Two hours later I was still watching Julie parade around in what must have been her six hundredth cocktail dress.

'Do you think they'll like this one, babe? I wore this one at the soap awards.' what she really meant was she'd worn it whilst hanging around the red carpet (behind security) outside the soap awards. "I've never been invited to a stag party before, see babes? God, I'm so excited. I have been to the odd stag do before mind, babes." She snorted and I really didn't want to go down the route of wondering why she'd been to stag do's. God, was I the only one who assumed a stag do was a bloke thing? 'But never one for two men and I've never technically had an invite.'

'Mam, can we have noodles for tea?' Davy was wearing sun glasses and a bobble hat. Today his t-shirt read; 'Take a minute! Risk assess.'

'Babes, you can have whatever. Give Mr Wong a ring. I'll have some prawn balls. I'm way too excited to cook with all these party plans floating around.'

Dread and disgust, together, are a mad combination of feelings! What was Dad playing at? He'd hated Julie's mad ways when he'd lived with us, called her all sorts of names, and now she was on the VIP list for this stupid bloody party.

'You want noodles, babes? Perhaps Mam would…'

'No. You're alright, thanks. Nan's done us spag boll. Thanks anyway though.' God, imagine Mam in here? Doctor A would definitely have to increase her medication dosage. (That is, if it could get any higher?)

'OK doll. Do you think this one will be alright then?' she twirled in what I can only describe as a flamingo fancy dress costume. The top half was all puffy and pink and the bottom half... well, there was no bottom half. Just very faked tanned orange legs in way too high heels. She finished the ensemble with some pink and yellow feathers in her already mad hair.

'Yeah, it looks really good.' Hey. At least someone would·look more mental than the groom to be and the groom to be.

The next morning it took me three attempts to book an appointment with the doctor. The first, I bottled it and immediately put the phone down. The second I accidentally hit redial dialling the last person who had called, who unfortunately for my panicked state, happened to be Crazy Nan. Phoning Crazy Nan under normal circumstances wouldn't have been a problem – if only I'd realised I was doing it.

'Hi can I book an appointment, please?' Nan, probably being drunk obliged, me being too nervous to recognise the slurring carried on.

'Yes dear. What for?'

'Well, I've...um...got a problem.'

'No worries my love. What sort?'

'Um...down below.'

'Oh, very serious. It was only last week I had some problems with down below too sweet heart.' My initial/ still incredibly nervous thoughts were; great a batty, elderly woman is telling me about her sexual exploits. Can things get any better? 'How did he contact you?'

'Um, well, it was an accident really, you see I was a bit drunk.'

'No problem dear. I also find he contacts me when I've had a drink. At first I thought it was the lord punishing me for enjoying a tipple but then I realised I was special. What would you like me to do about him?'

'I was hoping to see the doctor really.'

'Oh, luvvy, the doctor's can't do anything. If Satan wants you in hell he'll get you in hell.' Satan? Great she's religious; she thinks sex before marriage is evil.

'Yeah but I've read I can get cream. Can you just get me an appointment please?'

'Well, cream won't sort it but hang on I'll see what I can do. Hold the line.' if I'd been sharper it would have been the moment I heard a glass bottle hitting the table along with the phone. It was only when I heard; 'Ray!' did I click onto to who I'd actually phoned.

'There's a young man on the phone who's had a visit from the devil and wants some cream and a doctor. Is Barbara still dealing with that sort of stuff?' I immediately hung up. SHIT! As if crazy Nan needed any help. Barbara was her odd friend from bingo/spiritual church (The community centre gave them a discount if they held both events on the same night) Oh god, I hoped she didn't press 1471... too late.

'Hello?' too late.

'Hello dear, it's about the devil.' she whispered. 'I understand your embarrassed, but I know a lady.'"

'Nan? Is that you?' I crossed my fingers and made a mental note to thank God for half price bottled larger.

'JJ?'

'Yes Nan. What you on about?'

'Oh no! Has he got you?'

'No Nan, calm down.'

'But you just rang?'

'No I didn't. Nan, you must be confused.'

Silence.

'Yes, I must be. Sorry dear. Bloody Satan! I should have never given him my bloody phone number.'

'No Nan. Now go have some tea and a lie down.'

'Yes dear. I will. Sorry to have bothered you.' we respectively put our phones down and OK, I felt bad but I couldn't help grinning at the madness of it all. I then quickly and quietly booked an appointment at the surgery for two o clock.

Walking into the surgery was like having a not very pleasant outer body experience. I registered I was at reception, I even clocked onto the fact that Kaleigh Adams was in the waiting area but I seemed to click onto auto pilot.

'I've got an appointment at two.' I told the window in a normal voice.

'And?' the beast behind the desk was about one hundred and two and completely unpleasant she also smelled, worryingly, of primary school dinners and face paint.

'And I'm here for it.'

'With?' she had a long hair growing from her over made up chin.

'I don't know!' I felt my voice rising in pitch and loudness, but thee was nothing I could do about it. My inner angriness had taken over once again.

She sighed and shouted to someone called Shirley. After a little kerfuffle about files and rooms and the amount of Jones's registered at the surgery, Beast told me to 'take a seat,' I wasn't too pleased with her tone and to be quite honest and made a mental note to write an anonymous letter of complaint. Turning, a little too sharp-ish to be inconspicuous, I felt my face burn as I realised I'd have to (at all costs) avoid Kaleigh's corner, I mean last time I'd seen her I wasn't exactly pleasant. I took myself to what I hoped to be a dark corner. I then picked up a magazine and aimlessly leafed through it. It turned out I'd got half way through an article about the psychological effects of stretch marks on pregnant women when the unthinkable happened.

'Alright J?' now, I was beyond red. To be honest I imagined I was a perfect Dulux puce.'

'Kaleigh! Alright?' what a stupid thing to ask. If she was OK she wouldn't be in the bloody doctors. This flew through my brain too fast and the next thing to come out of my over active mouth was... (Drum roll)

'So, what you doing here?' oh god I wish someone would just cut my throat and let me die! I mean, look at why I was bloody there? An effin' STI for Christ sake.

'Sorry...I … I didn't mean to pry.'

'No, no it's OK. I think I've got a throat infection.'

'Oh right.' again my voice took on the pitch of an eight year old little girl whilst visions of not very nice things (if you know what I mean) in Kaleigh's throat went through my mind.

'So, what about you?' BANG! Right back at you JJ. I should have been prepared for that bad boy and of course it wouldn't have been an awkward question if I could only learn to fucking lie a bit better. There are thousands, millions even of reasonable explanations why a fifteen year old son of a gay man (not that, that fact even matters) could be at the doctors. Cold, flu, bad leg, infected finger nail the possibilities are endless. Of course my slightly hysterical/insane auto pilot mouth answered;

'My knobs not too good to be honest.' Kaleigh, firstly went pale, a complexion shade that was to rapidly change to her own version of puce. God, we'd have been an amazing advertising campaign for paint. She did a sort of giggle/ cough.

'Well, what I mean is… I've had this cold…' someone pass me the spade to dig a little deeper. '…and, its effected, like absolutely everything.' what was my fucking problem?

'You pregnant too?' she was smiling (that had to be a good sign, right?)

'God no!' I laughed in a manner that I hoped gave me back a little edge to my damaged persona. 'Not yet anyway.' I firmly shut the magazine and she giggled.

'Good, cause that would be bad news.' I smiled at her and a sort of awkwardness hung between us. Shit she was pretty. Nothing like that bastard chicken that had diseased my knob. OK, she was alright for a drunken rumble but nothing like Kaleigh- a proper lady like girl. I watched her fumble with a gold chain that was on her right wrist, (I couldn't help wonder whether a boy had bought if for her.) her eyes looked as if she wasn't sure where to look.

'Um...' she started and then monster from reception screamed;

'JONATHAN JONES. DOCTOR SING. ROOM FOUR. NOW!'

'That'll be me then.' I got up. 'See you round then?' *should I leave it like this?*

'Yeah, tidy.' she sat. I walked. And that was that.

Chapter Twenty-Seven

I was pleased to find out I had indeed caught a form of genital herpes. Marvellous! Getting my old boy out for Doctor Sing is a memory that, hopefully, will be eliminated from my memory bank. A bank full of tortured reminders of my pitiful existence so far. I'm hoping that pretty soon it'll be completely empty of my fifteenth year on planet Earth.

Anyway, the Doctor sent me packing with a pile of antibiotics, some smelly, smelly cream and lecture notes on the importance of contraception. He said I wasn't the first and certainly won't be the last.

I got home to find Mam had surfaced from her sedation period and was Mam 'not too good', but sort of normal. If she wasn't shaking so hard you'd never know she was ill. She was making coffee, in her dressing gown and reading the invitation I'd forgotten to hide.

'Are you OK?' I know she wasn't OK in the medical sense but I was hoping, sorry, preying, she was a little OK in the emotional sense.

'I suppose so. As OK as I can be considering I've been sedated for god knows how long and I've woken up to an invitation to my gay ex husbands stag *party*.' she really emphasized the *party* bit and let out a tired laugh, the type a divorced bi-polar middle aged woman does. My skin tingled as the hatred for my sperm donor surfaced once again. What was he playing at? Surely he could just get on with his life somewhere else so Mam and me could start rebuilding ours. Prick!

'Are you gonna go?'

'Of course not! Whoever heard something as crazy as an ex-husband inviting his ex-wife to his stag do to his new male fiancé? The mans turned gay and sick! I can't believe I didn't see it years ago? We were married for seventeen years – as you know- how come I never noticed it?' she smiled at me, to let me know she was OK.

'He's a knob Mam.'

'I know babe.' we both laughed and as the sun started shining into the room showing up the floating dust particles through the air, it was as if the tension old gay balls had created slowly started seeping out of the room. If only it was always like this? If he could just disappear and email every now and again, like Christmas and birthdays? God, think how easier things would be then?

'What about you, babe?'

'What do you mean?'

'Well, are you gonna go? He's still your Dad, knob or no knob or plus knob, even.' we both laughed again which gave me a second to consider my answer. Was I going to go? Doubt it, but as his bloody son did I have a duty to go? Last summer Ben Evans a boy in my math's class, got to go to Benidorm for a stag weekend. His Dad was getting re-married, to a woman mind, and him and loads of the valley's football boys flew from Cardiff. We were all mega jealous 'cause Ben said it was brilliant. He came back with photos of himself with topless women, who were really smart. He said they were strippers. I mean, that's what I thought a normal stag do consisted of? What the fuck was going to happen to an all male, literally, stag do that random neighbours and ex wives had been invited to?

'Earth to Jon, come in Captain Jones, come in.'

'Sorry Mam.'

'Thought I'd lost you for good then, babe.'

'No, I'm here. I was just thinking. Do you reckon I should go?'

'It's certainly a tough one. ..I think you'll have to do what's right for you, babe.'

'Well, I don't see anything bloody right with two fellas getting married, but I suppose it's a bit different when one of the grooms is your father.'

'Go for an hour? You may enjoy yourself.' she gave me a cheeky wink and I'd almost forgotten she was ill, was on tones of medication, had been in the nut house, that was until she said; 'You'll have to wear a dog collar mind babe, cause the Pope will probably be there wont he?' we both laughed again, although this time Mam wasn't sure what was so funny. Oh god, what a dilemma? If I didn't 'attend' was I making the situation worse, I mean who knows what lengths Dad would go to, to get me involved? But if I did go, well, what the fuck was likely to happen? Could I keep composed, or civil even? Could I even muster the strength to be polite in the first place? This debate battled on and on in my poor over worked brain until the Saturday evening of the so called party, where my actual attendance of the 'do' hit me with one hell of a bump, literally.

Chapter Twenty Eight

It wasn't a bang. More like a thud really. *Thud,* bump, bump, bump, silence. The cars headlights didn't even show Mike's rat like body on the road. He had landed too close to the bumper for proper showing.

It was the strangest of atmospheres in the seconds that followed. Everyone just seemed to stand still. Like bloody chess pieces. *Jesus.*

'Dad. Do something.' I don't know why the thought even crossed my mind that my useless dick of a father would start behaving like an adult now. I mean the idiots just seen his fiancée get run over by a boy racer and he's just stood there like a first class knob.

81

'Dad!'

The boy, who I instantly recognised as Tommy, Digger Dave's youngest son, scrambled out from the driver's seat of the sporty Renault.

'Is he dead? Oh God, he's dead isn't he? I've bloody killed him haven't I? My Mam's gonna murder me. Oh God.'

Of course, at this point everybody's still stood round like limp monkeys, so no ones actually sure whether Mike is breathing or not. If this was a film, there'd be some dead soppy piano music playing in the background, and me being the main man, hero even, would suddenly run to help the evil gay guy that brainwashed my Dad and save the day. (It would also be raining.)

In reality, I realised I couldn't actually give a shit whether Pansy Mike has just squeaked his last breath or not. Who would care? OK Dad may be a little distraught in the beginning but he'd soon come round. He may even realise the whole thing was a huge mistake and Mike is better off up there with all the other little poofter angels. He may even want Mam back?

My mind raced like this for quite a while, but then a terrible thought stabbed me in the conscience. What if Mike did die? Alright, yes that would be the easy answer to all the prayers I sent the Big Guy, but would it make me a murderer? I mean, it was me he was chasing, I was the last person who spoke, no sorry, screamed at him.

'Well officer the thing Is, we'd been on my Dad's stag-do. No, no, he's marrying Mike, the guy on the road. Yeah I know, weird isn't it? Well anyway, we were having a row, I ran off and the daft prick. Sorry, the idiot, chased after me and has obviously never read his green cross code, and threw himself on to the bonnet of Tommy's car.'

'Someone ring a poxy ambulance then.' my voice quivered which was another worry. I sounded bloody guilty.

My old man seemed to pull himself together and dial the three digits into his mobile. He practically screamed our exact whereabouts to the operator as he ran to his boyfriend, kneeling at his still body.

Now, I know I should have realised it before, but it was as my Dad stroked Mikey boy's hair, it clicked into my small, troubled brain how gay he actually was. God, before this I thought he was kind of pretending. I hadn't previously noticed his voice getting so high and girlie. I mean, I know he was a tad hysterical as he told Mike he 'bloody loved him, tumps and tumps' (Tumps? What the hell? Sick.) But he really did sound like a bender.

It wasn't that I doubted his feelings for Mike. After they moved in together I realised he was serious, just thought perhaps it was a phase of some sorts. You know? Everyone goes through some weird life crisis, take my Mam for instance? That poor buggers been through hell and back over the last couple of months, and OK it was all Dad's fault, but fair play the old girls pulled herself back.

'Come on baby boy, you can do it.' Well, the soft sod hit the nail on the head there. In fact, seeing Mike flat out on the concrete made him look dead young. Positively adolescent if I do say so myself.

'You alright, Kid?' my Dad asked.

Tommy was crying into some state of the art mobile phone (No doubt another knock off gift from his old man) and rubbing his real Burberry hat.

'JJ?' oh Christ he's asking me am I alright! Cheeky sod.

'Yeah fine.'

He shot me a look like he was about to kick off, but thankfully the flashing blue lights saved the day, literally.

I stood way back for the next bit. Oh yeah, way back out of sight, as the paramedics and police buzzed around quick and efficiently. As far as I could tell Mike still hadn't budged and Tommy had become irate, telling the coppers to F off and not to effin' touch him. At one point I definitely heard a comparison to a farm yard animal being screamed and the sound of a teenage boy directing a mouth full of gob in a particular direction.

The moments until the ambulance departed were a tad awkward to be honest. I was still loitering in the background like a train spotter whilst everyone sort of panicked. Obviously my old man went in the ambulance to the hospital and after the off I wasn't sure where to stand, how to behave or anything. At one point I did think about just handing myself into the coppers. But they're quite intimidating in they're force. (Especially when you're is feeling a little guilty)

Someone had rung Mam and strangely, she turned up with Doctor Atwood, the dude who looked after her in the nut house.

'Sweetheart, are you OK?'

God, why do Mam's always stroke your hair in a crisis? Not that I've been involved in many RTAs but when I broke my leg playing a cup game once. Mam had legged it on the pitch and stroked my hair as they carried me to the ambulance. She had then proceeded to rub my hair on the way to the hospital, whilst in hospital, on the way home from hospital and for the six weeks my leg was in plaster.

'Poor baby. You remember Graham hun?'

Doctor A, gave me a nervy nod, the type of greeting educated blokes do. I smiled and then I started to cry. God, I hate admitting it, but it was probably the relief of seeing Mam, someone who was on my side. The tears rolled down my cheeks as I sobbed and shook in her arms.

How had it come to this? An hour ago I was in the club wishing Mike dead and now I'm stood in what looks like a scene out of casualty, as my Dad's fiancée is being rushed to accident and emergency.

'What happened, baby?' Mam's tone was one of curiosity not conviction.

What a good question. What had happened? The stag-do had kicked off at seven. There were shit loads of fellas in the club. There was even some of those weird he/she things there. I'd never seen blokes with make up on before and to be honest I was slightly uncomfortable with it, but Julie from next door looked in her element, twirling round the… hims.   As the night progressed and I got some sneaky ciders, via Uncle Arthur, down my neck. I started to unwind, and all right it was probably intoxication but I even managed to be civil to some of Dad's odd, new friends. All was going well.

'They love your Aunt Marion see?' Uncle Arthur never really made much sense. But as he sunk several pints of mild, started spitting as he talked and stared at the barmaid's boobs, I hadn't a clue what he was on about.

'Peter the poof, from the Red Lion. Loves her he does. They probably talk about panties and lipsticks.' he laughed for about ten minutes straight before any sort of explanation was given. Even after I slipped in a couple of 'What you on about?' in between his giggles.

'Queers. They love her.' he rubbed his eyes and took a huge, high pitched breath. "Wherever we go there's a flock of um' following her around. When we went to Benidorm in March she picked up with a couple. Nice lads but bent as butchers hooks. One was a hairdresser, hence the fact she's got a bloody red fringe now. 'Do you like it?' she said. I mean, what was I supposed to say? Looks bloody ridiculous. Now your fathers bloody one of them.' he started to giggle again. 'Woo, doesn't make sense to me at all lad. You want another?' he nodded at my glass.

'Please.'

Well, at least there was cider to compensate this strange situation, these strange conversations and the even stranger people that were wandering round the club celebrating this farce of a wedding to be. God I wish I hadn't come.

And the hostility generally built up in this form until me and Mikey boy kicked off.

Now if you look up the word 'row' in the dictionary, the explanation given is; *an angry quarrel*. Which perfectly sums up mine and Mikes argument. As I said, I was being incredibly civil, keeping myself to myself, minding my own business. And then I caught sight of the arsehole, formally known as Mike. Who was fluttering around, licking my Uncle Dave's arse, even though Uncle Dave had no idea Mike was Dad's fiancée. In fact, Uncle Dave thought Dad's new partner was a bird called Sharon from up the valley. It was highly amusing to see Mike looking so puzzled when Dave asked how he was related to Shaz?

I was contemplating putting the record straight and considering the wonderful consequences (chairs flying, beer thrown, a possible blood injury?) when Mike said;

'Can I have a word, Babe?'

Now point one, I am certainly no *Babe*. What an insult. *Babe*. You don't call a fifteen year old boy *Babe*. What is the Ming Mong's problem? And point two, when the hell did he assume our relationship had developed to speaking terms. *Prick*.

'What?' was all I managed. My tongue was vibrating in my mouth. Aggression was not the word. I know my neck had gone red, the way it does when my tempers about to go, because suddenly my polo T-shirt felt way too tight around it.

'Outside OK?' outside? Why the hell did he want to go outside? And what if people see us leaving together? There is no way on God's earth I wanted anyone to see me even looking at Mike let alone engaging in a fully-fledged conversation with the knob.

The walk out of the club is a bit of a blur. To be honest I bet my eyes turned red. An evil red as I followed Mike's back through the flamboyant crowd. Isn't it funny how a human being can carry that much hatred for another person? I'm not talking about a dislike, I'm saying proper hate. Loathing, I mean, I despise this bloke with every cell in my body and now he wants to bloody chat. God, I hope he doesn't start crying or anything.

The Rugby Club car park leads straight out on to the main road. Once you're out of the big iron gates, whoop your right out there on the road that leads to the high street. Now, the actual argument was obviously predicted, but it was after a surprisingly civil conversation about vol-au-vents that it kicked off. I had made sure we had walked a safe distance, out of the car park and up the street a bit before we started, sorry let me correct myself, before the idiot pansy started.

'I need to get something off my chest.' he began. And I had to really hold my giggles in as I stared straight at the stupid silver chain he had round his neck. It was holding a huge pair of diamond wing things. It would have looked stupid on a girl, so you can imagine the effect it had on a very camp man, sorry, boy.

'I know you hate me, babe.' he was all hands and eyelashes as he spoke and I thought, Christ what is it with this idiot.

'Please don't call me *babe*.' I was so disgusted with the word I was tempted to spit it at him.

'Sorry. Um. Anyway what I want to say is that I really love your Dad. With all my heart. I mean that ...' his eyes started to glisten, which I think was down to one too many Spritzer's because his breath really smelt.

'... I've never felt this way before. Not even about Marco. He was an artist, my ex.' shut up! Shut up! Shut up! God, this bloke has got something wrong with him. Seriously. Did he even remember I'm his boyfriend's very hostile son? I didn't really take in the next part of the conversation. Just watched the dick head give the theatrical performance of his life. I occasionally registered the words love, marriage, big step, blah, blah, blah. Then he came out with it;

'The thing is, I haven't spoken to your Dad about it yet. Thought I'd see how you feel first. But when we're married, I'd really like to adopt you. Make us a real family unit. Can you imagine that? It'll be marvello. I can come and watch you play rugby, take you swimming if you like? It'll be great. You'll have two Dads'. Humph! I can't see your mother picking up with anyone else. Not after her little episode so you'll need a stable background.'

Wowa! Time, bloody, out. Did I just hear that right?

Adoption?

Now either I'm completely plastered, or I've fallen and banged my head, or the abducted by aliens theory has kicked in again and I'm actually in that parallel universe …

'So what do you think? A real little family. Oh imagine Christmas? I've always wanted a child of my own.' I really couldn't believe this. I mean, was this man a lunatic or what? I hate him and I'm pretty sure he's not overly fussed on me, and now he wants us to play happy families. Be a normal family with a stable background, don't make me laugh. How could we be a normal family, two benders and a son? Ha! Playing house and all. Christ they'd have me in twin sets and pearls, buying me Barbie dolls and fluffy kittens. Can you imagine?

'What are you laughing at, JJ? This wasn't the reaction I was hoping for.'

'Mike, do you really have to ask?'

Mike looked like he'd been kicked between the legs, and I'm sure his lip started to tremble.

'JJ, what's so funny? Don't you like the idea? I love your father and he loves you and I want us all to get along. I'll be his husband Jon so that technically makes me a type of father to you anyway. Don't you think it'll be better if it's, I don't know, official?' and I think this is the point where logical Jonathan Jones snapped. The hysteria abruptly stopped and anger kicked in. It was as if someone had injected me with adrenaline. My hands shook and my heartbeat resembled the most professional of tap dancing feet.

'Mike, I hate you. I even hate my own father because of you. I'm absolutely mortified that my Dad has chosen not only a prick, but a male prick to marry and now you don't only want me to grin and bare this messed up malarkey, you want me to be your bloody son? You are one strange herb.' I couldn't even look at the arsehole. I mean, how dare he even ask me. And all that bullshit about my Dad not knowing. I bet the dick put his pansy up to it.

'JJ please, at least think about it.'

'To be honest with you Mike, thinking about it makes me feel sick. You selfish bastards don't even know what you've put everyone through. I mean, you put my Mam in the nut house, I have no friends now, I even got bloody beat up because the two of you decided to shack up in the valley. You make me sick and I want nothing to do with you, either of you. As far as I'm concerned I don't even have one Dad anymore let alone two.'

And that was that. I turned my back on the near hysterical Mike and started to make my way towards town. I was aware of him screaming at me, the shuffling sound of his designer shoes on the road, then a squeak, which could have been Tommy's breaks or Mike screaming, then the thud.

'So I turned around to see Mike spread eagled on the road. Dad was stood on the opposite pavement just staring at him. Then he rang the ambulance.' I started to cry again then, so Mam stroked my head harder and harder until my sobbing eased.

'Sshhh baby. It's OK now, it'll all be alright, Mam's here.' I felt like such a child.

'Jonathan?' it was the policeman's tone that started the tears again, I suppose it was fear looking back. He had a really thick accent like he was from the city, not a valley boy. He'd never understand, I mean, they welcome benders down there with open arms, even dead manly policemen hang about with them in the trendy bars and that.

'Jonathan, it's alright I just need a couple of details off you. You're not in trouble.'

Now I've seen enough films to know that they always say that to the innocent blokes, that get framed in the end. You're not in trouble my arse.

'He' a bit shook up a minute, is there anything I can help with?' Mam had gone into efficient mode thank God, whilst I continued to crumble under the suspicious gaze of the scary policeman who was telling Mam that his name was Officer Gregory, and that he only needed contact details so they could get a statement once I'd calmed down.

'Erm, I think we'd better take you to the hospital, lad. Just to make sure you're all right, your pretty shook up. Understandably of course.' I'd forgotten Doctor Atwood was with Mam. He looked more nervous than me, poor bugger. I wondered why he was with Mam, God, I hoped she hadn't had a relapse that would really put the icing on this disgusting cake.

'Yes good idea. Perhaps someone can catch up with you down there. Get your statement then, save us traipsing to your house. Do you need a lift?' no way on Gods earth was I getting in a cop car that would be the end of my miserable existence; they might as well just drive me straight to jail.

'No its OK thanks. Grahams got the car haven't you hun?' Graham coughed and nodded and I couldn't help liking the bloke.

We went to the hospital in Doctor A's brand new Volvo, and if I hadn't been so distressed I would have been well impressed that he had a Stereophonics album on, in the built in CD player. I sat in the back, and to be honest I didn't take in much of the journey down. It was a warm night and Mam had her window down, the warm breeze made my head woozy. The smell of the country seeped into my nostrils as the car twisted through the lanes as we made our way down the Valley towards A and E. I would have given anything to have rammed my fingers down my throat and relieved myself of both the cider and the past four or five hours. But I didn't fancy staining the interior of the Volvo.

I hate the lighting in the waiting room of accident and emergency. It's a proper harsh light. Even in the car park the horrid glow through the windows isn't exactly inviting, and as soon as you're at reception the place hasn't got a very friendly atmosphere, despite the bright information board and play room.

As we walked through the steel automatic doors most of the stag-do seemed to be sprawled over the plastic chairs. Mam booked me in while Doctor A shuffled me to a free seat. God, I bet the hospital staff were confused, I mean, how do you explain this set up?

It took Dad about ten minutes to rear his ugly head. His face was stained with a red rash which meant he'd cried loads and I'm sure there was dried blood on his cheeks or it could have been make-up from one of his he/she mates.

'Alright?' he managed. His tone was angry and he couldn't even look at me. It wasn't as if Mike getting run over was my bloody fault. Daft sod should have looked where he was going. And Dad seemed quick to forget that all this was his bloody fault. He kneeled down and put his hands on my knees. In an instant I had jerked them away and my old man was flat on his back, spread out on the rubber floor. I didn't want him touching me. I didn't know where the dirty bastard had been for Christ sake.

'JJ, it doesn't have to be like this.' he whimpered. Mam made her way over to us and right on cue as she reached a spare seat, gay-boy Dad started blubbing like a baby.

'What the hell?' she asked. I couldn't take much more of this. How had it all happened? One minute I was milling around playing rugby with my friends, I had a sane Mam and a straight Dad. Now I'm in A and E sat with my nearly sane Mam and her mental Doctor (who could possibly be her boy friend) being blamed for my gay Dad's fiancée's accident.

'Is he alright? Mike, Is he OK?' again, thank the lord Mam had taken on the logical parental role.

'I, I, I don't know. They won't let me in there. Just rushed him into a room and ushered me out.' Dad really started making a show of him self then. Rocking back and fore on the floor, nearly screaming as he sobbed about not understanding how this could happen blah, blah, and blah. God, being gay really didn't suit him.

That night in the hospital was yet another strange one to add to my constantly increasing collection of strange nights. Slowly the sobering stag-do members gave their apologies and best wishes to Mike, but filtered out of the waiting room. Leaving only Doctor A, Mam, Dad and myself from that particular accident.

Being not such a high priority compared to a man with a whole pint glass embedded in his scalp, an old lady, who's hip had fallen out and an eleven year old girl, who's leg had turned the wrong way due to a nasty incident involving a game of cards, I wasn't seen by a Doctor until about three o clock. By which time Mam, Dad and poor Doctor A all looked slightly ill.

In the end, there appeared to be nothing at all wrong with me. Which made me wonder how some of those idiots acquired a PHD, or whatever they actually got. Alright, obviously at the time of the accident (Which felt like a million years ago) I was shook up. Who wouldn't be? Seeing someone get run over isn't exactly a pleasant experience I can tell you. But by three A.M the shaking had stopped, I'd sobered up and the whole incident didn't seem that bad.

'He's fine.' announced my Mam, as we came through the double doors, back to the waiting room.

'Not a scratch or bruise in sight!' she added to a very tired Doctor A and a practically dead gay Dad.

'That's great news.' Doctor A rubbed his palms down his cord trousers and as he got up I definitely heard several bones crack and click.

Dad was just staring at me. I couldn't make out what was going on behind his eyes. Did he hate me? Blame me for the accident? Or was he happy I was OK? Perhaps this whole things made him realise he doesn't love Mike, but even if he did that he loves me more and would hate to lose me?

'What Happened, Jon?' Oh. So there it was. The curiosity had got the better of the cat. He wanted the sordid details of the row, the argument that had got his beloved run over.

'What do you mean?' now I know you're probably thinking that I'm looking for another row or that I want to play the role of the awkward son. But genuinely, I needed to know exactly what he meant by 'What happened?' because at this stage of the game I couldn't afford to give anything away.

'What happened? Why had you walked away. What was so bad that you had to leave and he... he had chased you?' Dad's voice was still uncomfortably high pitched compared to his usual old tone and his words quivered like he was on the brink of tears, again!

'Dad, the thing is Mike...well Mike wanted...' so strange. My mouth had gone dead dry like I'd rubbed sand paper all in the inside of my cheeks, even under my tongue.

'Mike wanted ...'

'Mr Jones?' the double doors opened and out came a really important looking Doctor.

'Mr Jones?'

'Yes, that me. Is he OK? God, he's not is he?'

'Would you mind coming with me please, sir? So we can have a little more privacy.'

'Yes, yes of course. God it's not good is it?' as they walked back through those bloody double doors I heard Doctor Impressive ask Dad if he wanted a cup of coffee, which is always bad news on casualty, isn't it?

Waiting for the doors to re-open was like waiting for a bus when you're dead cold. There's nothing you can do about it but wait. Even though your body is numb with apprehension, your eyes start playing tricks on you and you can't think of anything other than the bloody thing turning up.

Doctor A drunk about eight cups of coffee and had started to shake in the time we waited for Dad to re-emerge. Mam kept tapping his knee and smiling at him in a way I hadn't seen her smile before. Even though she was quite clearly knackered she looked, I don't know, sort of younger. Happy even. And it was just before Dad came back through to the waiting room that it hit me, exactly how strange love is. And even stranger who falls in love with who. Take Dad and Mike, I mean I hate it, I hate everything about them being a couple, but I doubt they planned it. They hadn't set out just to piss me off. They had fallen hook, line and sinker for each other. I wonder was it even about fancying each other? Dad obviously fancies Mike a bit or they wouldn't hold hands and stuff but perhaps they just clicked on a level where they had to, I don't know, develop their friendship maybe?

Wow! I was just considering how things click into place (and I'm not talking Lego. I'm talking the big picture, the whole wide world type of thing) When Dad came through the doors and the look on his face said it all.

I couldn't bring myself to say anything. To be honest, I couldn't even look at him. What had I ruined? Okay. I was along way from acceptance but I think I was close to the start of adapting to Dad's choices. I mean, I was still really uncomfortable with the fact he was gay, lets just say I wouldn't go boasting about it, but if he was happy, in reality, who the hell was I to stand in the way?

'What happened? What did they say?' again, Mam was first to take the reins.

'He's badly hurt. He's lost a lot of blood.' Dad spoke like he was on automatic pilot. He'd gone pale and was shaking, I felt sick, sick to the stomach.

'Will he be alright though?' Mam was so sensible, even after everything Dad had put her through she was concerned.

'He needs a blood transfusion. Quickly.'

'Well, that should be easy enough, shouldn't it?' of course, Graham, or Doctor Atwood was trade, wasn't he?

'It's not that simple.' Dad sunk to his knees (yet again!) and started to whimper.

Once, I saw a puppy get run over. It was the most horrible thing I'd ever seen. I was on my bike and I watched as the bundle of fluff tugged out of its collar and bounded across the road. There was nothing the driver could have done. She was a young girl and after she'd slammed her breaks on, she had bolted from the car, straight to the puppy. Of course the poor little thing hadn't stood a chance against a Toyota Yaris, but the driver cuddled the corpse for ages, whimpering. Just like my Dad was on the hospital floor.

'Dad?' he looked up at me. Tears fell uncontrollably from his swollen eyes. 'Dad, it'll be OK.'

Now, you'll probably think I've gone crazy, because earlier I wouldn't let the bloke touch me. But, after all he's still my Dad and I knew once I had the urge to console him I should just do it. So I too, lowered myself to the floor and for the first time since this horrid mess had begun I hugged my father. Don't get me wrong I was still hoping, for the love of god that no one I knew caught me, but the bloke obviously needed to be consoled. So, he cried in my arms and I considered how a transfusion couldn't be that simple.

I took Dad a weak cup of machine-made earl grey, (whatever that is) a sneaky gin from Mam's even sneakier hip flask and probably two and a half tear stained toilet rolls before he started to make any sense. And to be honest even then he spent most of the time banging on about how much he loved Mike and how young he was and even how there couldn't be a god because anyone with a heart wouldn't have caused such a bad accident, blah, blah, blah. Basically, the long and short of it was that Mike had one of those rare blood types or some shit, which, really wasn't as bad as initially thought. I wasn't sure of the mathematics (never has been my strong point)   of the procedure but apparently according to the doctor, a nurse and the bloody receptionist drama queen Dad had had one too many Martini's and over reacted at the diagnosis. The doctors attempt to pump coffee into him hadn't been to brace the dick for bad news but to sober him up!

When he did eventually, did sober up the clock in the waiting room area wasn't a pretty sight. Eight forty five to be precise and dead is the only word to describe how I was feeling. I'd managed to (nearly) fully explain my side of the story, conveniently missing the adoption bit out completely. And thank god everyone bought that I'd just told Mike to leave me alone, I'd turned, he'd followed and BOOSH! Stage enter Tommy's boy racer. Anyway, it was Mam who suggested we make our way back to home and a caffeine'd to the max Doctor A, shook his head in agreement, or just shook in general, I wasn't sure.

Dad refused point blank to leave, as Mike, after having his very 'rare blood' transfusion, was due to wake any time soon. Mam vowed to call back after a nap and some breakfast and Doctor Atwood mumbled something along the lines of; 'I hope he gets better.' Although, don't quote me on that.

I've always been a bit of a romantic. Now, I know I should never, ever under any circumstances admit that type of information out loud, but seriously I'm a fan of nice endings, happily ever afters and all that bollocks! I suppose with Dad being a bender at least I know where I get it from. Let's just hope (apart from the nose and being left handed, which are technically out of my hands!) that's where the similarities end. Anyway, getting back from the hospital at stupid o clock in the morning my already confused perspective on love took a dramatic turn for the... well, I'm not entirely sure. Doctor Atwood swung his Volvo onto our drive and as he put his foot on the middle pedal, I picked up on a sudden change of atmosphere, but it wasn't until

Mam asked me to 'go on into the house babe.' that I realised I seemed to have taken the role of a big fat gooseberry!

Taking up a not-so-amazing hiding place between the blinds I saw Mam smiling, waving, her hands (obviously explaining something...medication maybe?) giggling (definitely medication) and kissing... oh my god! There was my Mam engaging in full on tongue action with the mental doctor in his Volvo! Surely that was slightly un-ethical on his part? I mean, she's crazy for Christ sake. And then I had another bang of realisation right between my eyes straight into my brain. Mam had moved on. With all that had happened she'd picked herself up, dusted herself off and got straight back on the horse again, so to speak. To be honest, at first I was slightly miffed, I mean, how could she just sit in the drive and snog doctor? 'poor me' rang through my head until I realised how selfish I was being and decided; surely Mam deserved some bloody happiness and who the hell was I to stand in her way? And at least if she was banging the doctor, she'd probably always have a vast supply of medication/sedation stuff/straight jackets or whatever bi-polar sufferers need these days. And another massive plus point being I wouldn't have to take the brunt of the bad days, maybe even, Doctor A would take full responsibility for Mam. Ooh, what if they decided to get hitched? That would take the shine off Dad and Mikes nuptials for sure.

I started doing my action Mam impression across the living room floor so Mam wouldn't know I'd been spying, when the door clicked and I realised Mam hadn't come in on her own.

'Come through officers. We've only now this minute got back. I was just thanking Doctor Atwood for the lift. On the drive. Out there.' Mam did a high pitched sort of laugh then.

So they'd come to arrest me. Great stuff! I was going to be framed for the suspected murder of my Dad's boyfriend. (God it still didn't sound right, *boy-friend*!)

'JJ! Where you to babe? He came in just before me.' the door creaked and in they came to witness me dragging myself along the floor. Yeah, I was the personification of not guilty!

'JJ, what you doing babe?'

'I fell. Well, I dropped something and then I fell to look for it. Oh, you know what I mean. I'm on the floor looking for what I dropped, hello yous two's.' now I looked (in no particular order) guilty, cocky and fucking mental.

'Alright Son?' oh yeah, I'm fucking marvellous buddy. You think I tried to murder gay boy Mike, Mam's not only crazy but shagging the bloke that diagnosed her, and here I am clawing my way across Mam's poxy wooden floor whilst you two got bloody accusation written all over your faces! Things really couldn't be much better! Of course what I said was;

'Um, yeah. Tidy thanks.'

'Well son, if you'd like to get up we'd like to get a statement off you. It won't take long, son.' God, it really was like a version of a modern bloody heartbeat with little and bloody large. Or like the bill – valley style-y!

Now, I know technically, I should be sucking up to the 'force' however my adrenalin had other ideas and once again my mouth moved faster than my brain, my very, very tired brain I might add.

'Look, it wasn't my fault. He's a twat…'

'J! Watch your mouth.'

'Well, he is Mam. He's an absolute …'

'OK sonny. Slow down.' I'd moved from slithering across the floor (face down, ass up) to upright and pacing. For god's sake none of this was my fault and how dare everyone intimidate and blame me, how dare these knobs come into my house and start clogging my brain with court scenes and detention centres. It is not my fault that people don't accept queers!

'Now, we just need a statement from you.'

'I DID NOT PUSH MIKE INTO THE CAR!' the thin copper rubbed his eyes. He looked way to puny to be a copper. In fact, he looked alarmingly like an older version of the bloke that drives the ice cream van round, the one from the estate.

'... We've just spoke to your Dad, and we know you didn't push him sonny, we just need your version of the events. It's for procedure purposes. Make sure everyone's story fits into place for the paperwork.'

Then the other one started.

'So if you can just tell us what happened and we can let you catch up on your sleep. I'm sure you're both very tired.'

Wowa! Time out! Now I was in a predicament. What exactly had Mike said? What should I say? Maybe I should just say I didn't see anything, that it all happened too quickly for me? Or I could just tell the bloody truth! Because the truth was the truth, I was innocent it was all just a nasty accident.

So that's what I did. I replayed the whole tedious accident, from Mike's stupid necklace making me giggle to him asking to adopt me which made Mam giggle and the fat copper grin. Don't get me wrong the fuckers probed quite a bit but I think it was just to guarantee all parties stories matched, not to frame yours truly!

It wasn't until the pigs had gone and Mam had started to put some breakfast on did I start really thinking about the events of the last two days or so. I mean, don't get me wrong, I'm certainly not giving the pair of mad bastards my blessing but god, they must be serious about each other for Mike to even consider voicing the adoption idea? And the stag party wasn't actually to make a prick out of me, but to show everyone they were a couple that meant business. Which made me have to admit they defiantly had balls – literally, more balls than any other couple round here. And for the first time since they'd announced their engagement I thought; good on them! They'd found something that went against the grain, and gone ahead and got what they wanted, bollocks to everyone else. And okay that was including me but I haven't exactly had it that bad, have I? they haven't beat me or starved me, I've suffered no abuse, I've only really been loved. So why was I causing such a bloody fuss? I mean it was no ones business but theirs, was it? Fuck everyone else.

And it was at that moment, I changed my tune. Just like that.

Chapter Thirty

A banana is technically a berry, a herb, a fruit and a plant all at the same time. They are propagated asexually from offshoots of the plant, not seed. So, if something as simple as a banana can be so many things, it is of no surprise that Dad once fancied Mam and now he's getting married to Mike, is it?

PART TWO

Chapter Thirty-One

Mike got better. In fact, he was rapidly back to very camp Mike in no time at all. I went to see him and Dad in the hospital the day after the police took my statement. And okay, it was difficult for me to be instinctively warm and embracing, they were still having it up the arse for God's sake, but I think they could tell something had shifted. And it had, my hostility towards them had more or less disappeared.

And although happy is quite a strong word, seriously I was sort of happy-ish for them. And Dad was pleased to have me back in his life for sure. It took Mike a while, as in twenty seconds, but even angry Mike was still overly positive.

'Oooh, I'm loving your top, JJ.' he said it with his arms crossed and never meeting my eyes which, I didn't mind because the last time he'd seen me we'd had an almighty argument which resulted in him getting knocked over.

'It's good of you to come, son.' Dad had washed and changed and looked quite healthy considering the state he'd been in a couple of hours before.

It didn't take long for the initial awkwardness to disappear and for two gay men and an adolescent to find some common ground to bond on, or so to speak.

Right, when I say common ground, I mean, firstly we talked about the party, (carefully missing out the argument and accident) then we mentioned the drunkenness of Uncle Arthur (carefully missing out his homophobic tendencies) Then we got talking about Mam and Doctor Atwood (definitely missing out whether they are, indeed, pumping) and, before I knew it we were laughing and making jokes – all boys together. And, if I'm honest I'd totally forgotten the fact they were partners. That was until Mike said;

'Babe, have you sorted the castle?' Dad shot Mike a look and gave me an 'I'm sorry' sort of smile.

'It's OK. You can talk about the wedding.' check me out being all grown up, or should I say mature?

'Really?' Dad looked concerned. I mean, what on Earth did he think I was going to do? Bump Mike off? (Sorry, bad joke)

'Yeah. Course you can talk about it. It's quite a big deal, And, I figured you are my Dad after all.' They both started beaming. 'But, just don't go ramming it down my throat, OK?'

'No problemo, Kiddo.' I started to smile; he used to say that before…before…well, before he got with Mike. Same Dad, different taste.

'So, do you wanna be page boy, or something?' Mike's eyes were all sparkly the way Mam's get when she sees nice shoes in the catalogue that she can't afford.

'No!' Dad sounded angry. 'JJ, I know you'll probably hate the idea, and I don't expect an answer straight away, but, I'd love you to be my best man, kid.' Mike gasped and put his face in his hands, and for a minute I thought we'd have to call a nurse and then I realised, he really should have gone to stage school.

'I don't need to think about it Dad, I can't believe you're even asked, your so insensitive.' kicked puppy look; activated. 'The thing is I'd just assumed I'd be bloody best man.'

'I'm sorr…what did you just say?'

'I said I'd assumed I'd be best man, Gay Boy.' and with those two words hanging in the air, I felt like I'd just tested a new deodorant in a busy shop. And I wasn't sure whether Dad and Mike liked the smell of it. I wasn't sure where I'd found this new brave attitude. And then the partners started to laugh and so I joined in until I was clutching my stomach and wiping tears from my crumpled up face.

A couple of days later I found myself in crazy Nan's tiny living room along with the happy, healthy couple that had become the Nan's answer to Sir Elton and David what's his face, Mam and Doctor Atwood who were looking like teenagers, (and I bet your thinking I've got a cheek, but seriously they looked like kids in my class) Nan, of course and Bamp, and also for some absolutely mental reason Julie and Davy from next door.

We all had been summoned for one of Nan's Sunday roasts which consisted of about, a thousand Yorkshire puddings, and microwavable chicken Kormas which were given to us in the black plastic trays they came in. Oh yes, there were also about twenty bottles of Tescos value wine on the table and several crates of Stella under the table for when the wine runs out, and run out it would.

I've got to be honest, at first I was a little dubious about a 'family bonding session' as Nan had labelled it. I mean, I'd only just got my head round the whole, having a gay father issue, wasn't it a tad soon to be playing happy families? God, imagine us lot on a quiz show, how the hell do you go about explaining this set up?

'Back in tomorrow, is it boy?' Bamp, was pottering around awkwardly. He obviously was still a bit weary of the whole gay transition thing on Dad's part. Probably because he wasn't on as such Valium as Nan, who evidently was gushing over Mike; 'we've always wanted an extra son' she kept telling Julie between massive mouthfuls of wine from a mug.

'Yeap. GCSE's this year, Bamp.'

'GCS what lad? Is that slang for some sort of crew? I been watching stuff on Sky about crews. You mind your back, homey?' Bamp started to crack up whilst Mike looked slightly put out.

'Oh J, are you one too babe? I read it was genetic.' Julie looked curious.

'No. No, I'm not Julie.' I looked pissed off.

'Course he ent' Mam. Homey, you know? It's what Americans say en it?' Davy looked embarrassed.

'So, it's not short for a home-o-sexual, then, issit?'

'Ma, how many have you had?' Dad looked cross.

'Leave off of her, son. She's had a lot to deal with, with you two carrying on.' Bamp avoided eye contact.

'And what's that supposed to mean?' Mike looked angry.

'It means…'

'We're getting married to.' Everyone's heads spun like owls over to Mam and the Doc. Married? God, he'd only diagnosed her like, a couple of months ago and now they were getting married? Shit, was everyone on drugs or something?

Nan and Julie started applauding and Mam flashed a little diamond around the room. How come I hadn't noticed that? God, I really must learn to start paying more attention to things that don't revolve around my father's sexuality.

I was deep in thought considering whether everyone had actually been abducted by some sort of romantic Aliens when I heard Nan's patio doors slam and the weird beaded curtain bang across the glass.

Mike was sulking. Mike was in Crazy Nan's garden sulking like a big baby. When he saw me he theatrically wiped his big brown eyes, sighed and crossed his legs.

'Sorry Babe.' God, when would he learn not to call me fucking babe? It was going to be really hard for me to keep up this civil alliance if he kept referring to me as one of his pets!

'Mike!'

'Sorry J. I meant to say *Fella.*' he really pronounced 'fella' like someone who'd once been a woman but had had Jerry Springer 'I'm now a man' operation.

'That's okay Mike, you're alright.' he did another massive sigh before lurching into an, I'm very sorry for myself, speech.

'She's upstaged me. I'll always be in her shadow. Sorry JJ, I know she's your mother.'

'I don't think Mam could ever upstage you to be honest Mike, I mean, they'll be two completely different weddings I should think, wont they? Well, unless you'll be wearing a dress and Dad grows a beard?' Mike started hooting.

'God, J you crack me up *bay*...buddy. It's, just sometimes ...god, I'm not sure whether I should even be saying this to you J, but...'

'Go on Mike.'

'Well, it's just. I'm not sure about everything...with your Dad. I mean, I love him, honestly JJ I think the world of him but how can I compare to what he had with your mother and you!'

'You can't Mike. But, that didn't exactly work out did it? And honestly, I doubt Dad would have made all this fuss about the wedding and everything if he wasn't serious about you.' Mike wore a perplexed expression and it took a while for my words to digest with him. He was just about to say something when the patio doors opened and Dad lumbered out onto the lawn.

'If you'd told me a month ago that you two would be as thick as thieves in my Mam's back garden I'd have thought I'd had more chance winning the bloody lottery.' Mike let out a nervous giggle, as if we were discussing something illicit which made me feel slightly uneasy, although I was getting fed up with this paranoia lark.

'Well, I'll have you know Mr Jones, me and your son are getting on fabulously, right J?'

'I hate to admit it, but we're okay. But he is closer to my age Dad.'

'You cheeky shit.' we all had a laugh in the garden for a while before Nan informed us that 'grub' was 'up!' And after our curry's and Yorkshires and the empty bottles began to mount up, talk turned to weddings. It was mad! Mam and Dad both swapping wedding notes. I mean, they'd had one of their own not so long back.

'Why don't you have a joint one, kids?' nice one Nan. As if I wasn't going to get enough stick at school tomorrow without having two gypsy style bloody weddings to attend. God, if I wasn't already an outcast with all this scandal surrounding me, I was definitely about to become one-again!

Chapter Thirty-Two

The first day back at school wasn't too bad. It was the second when things started to rapidly go down hill. OK, so I've been through quite a bit already so a bit of banter off my boys is nothing. In fact, it's expected, isn't it? It's shit off dinner ladies that took the piss to be honest.

I was queuing for a well deserved heap of carbs (GCSE's are tougher than I expected.) when I found my usual favourite dinner lady (Marion) to be quite rude, and when I use the word 'quite' I'm using it very loosely. Firstly, she grunted, which was an indication for me to tell her what I wanted.

'Chips, cheese and beans, please Mar, with a bread roll as well.' was my answer, with my best smile, in a chirpy voice, I'd like to add. She grunted again then tottered off muttering something, I couldn't quite make out, under her hairnet. Approximately ten minutes later, which is a long time in an only forty-five minute dinner hour, and several hungry kids behind me, nice old Marion practically throws a measly portion of what looked like chips, cheese and beans the sequel, at me.

'Um, thanks.' she then sort of hissed at me before asking the kid behind me;

'What can I get for you my darling?'

'JJ, what the fuck is on your plate?' never one to beat around the bush, even if he did have a massive mouthful of something I couldn't identify, Wedgy looked disgusted.

'Well, it's meant to be…'

'Don't tell me. It's pank, right?'

'What the fuck is pank?' Meeky was ramming forkfuls of meat into him. He's pure man is Meeky, thinks anything vegetable based is girly food and honestly believes pasta is food that Father Christmas's elves eat.

'You've never heard of pank boys?'

'Course we have. That's why we're all asking you what it is, you fucking plank.' Meeky, also never one to mince his words.

'Well, maybe you should be asking JJ boys. I'm sure he knows what it is. Ey J?'

'Now, what the fuck have I done?'

'Well chicken, you've had a first hand experience of pank, Boyo.' and the banter generally went from shagging a chicken, to catching 'bird bloody flu', to having a father that's marrying another fella and so on. But I could handle the boys.

'Ey, why do you reckon Marion just threw my so-called pank at me, then?'

'Did you change your mind a lot? She tends to get mad if you keep changing your order.'

'No.'

'Oooh, did you say your food looked like pank?'

'No.'

'Did you tell her she had a nice arse?'

'No. yuck.' we all shot Wedgy before laughing for quite a while.

'Serious boys? What do you think I've done? I hate it if I've pissed someone off.'

'Arrr, bless JJ's showing his soft side.' Meeky gave me a wink, cheeky sod.

'Don't now.' I couldn't help grinning. Fair play since they'd had it out with me (well, after they'd beaten me up) they'd also just got on with the fact Dad's a bender and it had jack shit to do with me. In fact, this morning before registration, in the cloakroom they'd told Debbie Davies, or rent-a-mouth as she was known, to fuck up and fuck off. We' overheard her telling her posse of girls that Dad was shagging a bloke. Mind, I wonder how long this alliance would last now I'd signed myself up for best man duty?

'JJ, do you think she's one of those people?' I thought Wedgy's eyebrows were about to fall off, he was moving them so much.

'One of what people dickhead, a dinner lady?' I knew immediately what sort of person Wedgy was on about. The type of person we all were before all this, they type of people everyone in the Valley was and Marion was not the first and probably wont be the last I was gonna meet now Dad was well and truly out of the closet.

'You know…' Wedgy searched the table for back up.

'Yeah, the thought had crossed my mind buddy.' and it had, but only briefly, because Marion didn't strike me as judgemental.

'Will someone tell me what the fuck you're on about?' Meeky, Man, straight to the point and impatient.

'Well, Marion don't like our boy here cause, well cause…'

'Because she thinks I'm GAY!' I hadn't meant to shout. Honest.

'Nah, she ain't like that, is she?'

'Apparently so, you want dessert J. I'll get it for you in case you end up with regurgitated custard?'

'No ta, butt.'

'Well, you should tell someone, the head, or something? Its wrong man, it's not your fault your old man takes it up the arse.' then it was my turn to laugh, god these boys had seriously short memories. 'What's so funny?'

'Meek, look how you reacted when you found out, you broke my ribs!'

'Yeah, but that was different, mate. I thought, well, I thought you was one too, didn't I?'

'Exactly, perhaps Marion does?'

'NO. You don't look like one, do you? And she doesn't exactly have to take showers with you does she?'

'No I don't, and my Dad doesn't look like one either.'

'True. And true. But even if she did think you was, you know?'

'Gay?'

'Yeah, even if she did think that, there's no bloody need to throw shit food at you. You're not diseased like, are you?'

'It's not really as simple as that though, is it? I mean, as far as people like her are concerned I am one hundred percent contaminated with the GAY gene.'

'Are you?'

'Fuck up Wedgy.'

Later that afternoon, during a very boring compulsory religious education lesson, I got to thinking more about Marion and her blatantly shit behaviour. I mean, why was I being punished for my old man's choices? Especially in the canteen, that was way below the belt in my eyes. It took me forty five minutes of pure pondering to decide that I was going to see Marion, bugger maths last lesson, I wanted to know what the fuck was going on and whether I'd have to start bringing a packed lunch.

She was sitting with a herd of other dinner ladies in the canteen, drinking from mugs and eating biscuits. What a job! I couldn't help but wonder whether they were getting paid for just sitting round nattering or whether they'd had to pay for their tea? Technically all I was doing was avoiding what I really had to think about – a task made even harder by the look Marion gave me as I walked in. it was a look that went unrecognised by her serving crew as the hall fell silent.

'Um, Marion can I have a word please?'

'I'm busy Jonathan.'

'Well, it's sort of important.' she looked disgusted. And I felt the muscle in my forehead begin to throb. What was this woman's problem? God, it had to be more than Dad's coming out surely? I mean, no ones that childish are they?

'Five minutes.' she got up and I followed her fat-aproned-arse out into the hallway.

'Marion, have I upset you?' like ripping a plaster off, quick and painful!

'It's just so wrong on so many levels. Its disgusting that's what it is.' she couldn't even look me in the eye.

'Look, I'm not exactly overjoyed by the whole set up but, its nothing to do with me, so don't take this the wrong way but it's nothing to do with you either.'

'It is everything to do with me sonny Jim. He's broke my daughters heart, left her with two kiddies and a mortgage and muggings here is picking up the pieces, so I think you'll find it has everything to do with me . My living room is full to the brim with their stuff so the bailiffs don't get it.'

Time out! What the hell was she on about? Mike has broken Marion's daughter's heart or had Dad? Mike really doesn't strike me as ever being capable of raising children or even raising his anatomy for a woman and I'm sure I would have heard if Dad had shacked up with Marion's daughter?

'If I catch hold of him there'll be murder. Bloody cheek of him, call himself a bloody doctor. Doctor my arse.'

'Marion, what are you on about?'

'I'm on about your mother running off with my Lesley's, Graham. She must have a heart of stone, bloody mare.' oh my God! Doctor 'saint' Atwood had/has a wife!

'So, this has got nothing to do with my Dad?'

'You're Dad? No nothing, I don't think.'

'So, it's not cause he's gay then?'

'Good god no. I met his boyfriend or partner or whatever he is in Tescos last Saturday.' her face softened. 'Lovely couple, nothing like your mother mind, I always knew she was a bit loose.' Jesus Christ I was not expecting that.

'Marion, I'm really sorry about all this, but it's nothing to do with me. So, I'd really appreciate if you'd leave me out of it all.' as I walked away my brain couldn't process what had just happened. So, I wasn't having crap food because Dad's gay but because my Mam has stolen someone's husband. Bloody hell fire. With only twenty minutes or so to home time I decided to skip maths completely and go pay Dad a visit, he'd probably be able to make some sense of this crazy situation.

I hadn't actually been to Dad and Mike's love shack, (the thought still made me shiver a bit) but I knew where it was. When I knocked the door I wasn't sure whether I'd made the right decision coming here, I mean, okay we were all on talking terms, but was I being slightly disloyal to my

Mam? And, what if I was imposing? God, what if they were doing something, something I really didn't want to walk in on? Oh hell! I was just about to do an about turn, when Dad opened the door.

'J, buddy, you alright?'

'Hiya. Just thought I'd pop round, but you're probably busy so I'll…'

'No, no come in, you hungry? I'm making lasagne be about an hour but I'd love you to stay and have some.'

'Actually Dad, I'm starving.'

'Come in than, Kid.'

Dad and Mike had set up home in Eureka Place. A terraced street that has loads of three storey houses and fair play to the boys they'd done their abode up quite nicely if I do say so myself. There wasn't a trace of pink or fluff or anything remotely camp and to be honest their house was nicer than Mam's although I feel terrible admitting that. God, I really was going to get the terrible son award this year. Dad took me down to the basement, where they had a massive steel kitchen. Mike was at the breakfast bar and was wearing a pair of glasses, which made him look a little bit older and quite intelligent.

'J, God, what a nice surprise. You are staying for tea?' you couldn't knock gay people's hospitality that was something.

'Yeah. If that's OK?'

'Course it is. You're always welcome here.' Mike began cleaning his stuff away and I managed to catch a glimpse of some of his photographs, and I must have let my eyes linger too long because Mike said; 'They're just some test shots for my finals.' he blushed and continued to put them in massive files.

'They look really good.'

'They are. He's very secretive about them though.' Dad was grinning and it was a bit creepy but I couldn't have a turn because I was in they're house and I was too hungry to leave before the lasagne.

'I am not... Well, they're personal.'

'I'd love to do something like that.' and I did mind, I wasn't just being polite, I've always liked creative stuff it's just its a bit girly ain't it?

'I can show you one day, if you like?'

'Yeah alright, If you don't mind, like.' and it was as easy as that. The awkwardness had officially gone and as long as they don't start snogging or getting touchy I could cope with it all.

'There we are then. I'm gonna get dinner on.' Dad looked pleased as punch, so I wondered whether now would be a good time to mention Mam and the Doctor? I didn't really want to bring the mood down but I couldn't really talk to anyone else about it.

'You don't have onions, do you kid?'

'No evil, slippery, things.' Dad laughed.

'I'll leave em' out then. So, how are things, school alright?'

'First week back is always crap.'

'Yeah but it's the start of the season, ent it?'

'Yeah.'

'J, are you alright really?' Dad plopped his pots and pans down and I sighed.

'It's a bit awkward really Dad.'

'J, we've been through quite a lot the past couple of months so, surely you can tell me whatever's bothering you.' true. So, I thought, bugger it. I told Dad everything about Mam's new bloke, well; everything that Marion had told me. And, it felt good, to just unburden myself and to be honest it felt good to have two parents again, even if one was gay and the other bloody crazy.

Chapter Thirty-Three

Walking home from Dad's I tried to take his advice on board. I'd forgotten how logical he could be and I was feeling quite relived to have a bloke to talk to again, even if he was gay. He'd told me not to worry about Mam's love life, easier said than done, he'd said, but I suppose he had a point, I mean, really it was nothing to do with Mam or me whether Doctor A had left a wife and family behind. Mam had hardly stolen him away, had she? She didn't seem in the frame of mind to go stealing husbands really. She didn't seem in the frame of mind for anything normal to be honest.

I was deep in thought processing all the positive points of Mam's new love life when I got that really weird feeling, as if there's someone right behind you. Now, I know I'm a pretty paranoid person, but seriously I'm sure I could hear footsteps and everything! So, I quickened my pace, I mean, I'd already had one hiding and an STI, so I really didn't fancy being attacked or raped or whatever this psycho had in store for me.

'J, wait up.' I recognised the voice immediately. Oh Juliet! 'What you running for?'

'Well...it's a long story. Thought you were, well thought you were someone else. You alright?' Mumbling and blushing very attractive JJ. Fucking hell this girl had one hell of a hold over me.

'Yeah, I'm good. We're in different English classes this year, then?'

'Oh, I hadn't noticed.' of course I had. I was hopeful for the first lesson that she'd been late or maybe ill. By the third lesson I was blatantly gutted!

'Yeah, I was hoping we'd be in the same one because it's the only lesson we get, or got together and we used to have fun, didn't we?' oh, she's so pretty. I'm talking perfection here, and this is no bull shit, I swear to you, the sun shines on her in a particular way, I mean, she's an angel, honest. I reckon if I looked close enough (which I don't want to in case I look creepy) even her freckles would be in the shape of stars.

'Yeah, it was a laugh, where you off then?' she'd changed out of her uniform and was wearing a pair of cut off jean things and a white vest which made her breasts look lush. God, what I wouldn't give to hold them. I wouldn't even mind if she kept her bra on.

'Just up the park, to see the girls.'

'Oh, tidy.' I didn't want to say; 'Oh, why don't me and you do something?' this girl makes me turn to fucking mush, seriously I'm absolutely useless around her.

'Where you off still in your uniform?' oh shit she pulled my tie. I felt JJ junior stir. Holy shit! This has got to be love!

'Just been to see my Dad.'

'You're talking, that's mega.'

'Yeah, after the accident and everything, I decided life's to short.'

'I did hear about all that. Its really good you're talking anyway.'

'Yeah, he's asked me to be best man at his wedding or civil ceremony or whatever it bloody is.' I laughed, partly because the whole thing still seemed a bit ludicrous and partly because I couldn't believe I'd just told Kaleigh Adams, the coolest, prettiest girl I've ever known that I'm about to be best man at a gay bloody wedding.

'That's amazing. Wow. What a privilege. I'd love to see you in a suit.' she was definitely flirting. Definitely, definitely.

'You could come with me? I mean, my invite says 'Jonathan Jones and guest'' I hadn't even had the invite yet, but that's what all invites say, don't they? 'I mean, only if you fancy it, don't feel like you've got to come or anything?'

'Jon, I'd love to. Just let me know where and when and I'm there, in a frock!' I was beaming. That's the only way I can describe my outsides and insides.

'Tidy.'

'Well, do you fancy doing something on the weekend? Perhaps we could go to Cardiff on the train? Bit of shopping, something to eat, we can plan the wedding arrangements, is it?'

Oh my god! Shopping and food, this would not only be a date but we'd be like a couple, a real couple!

'Yeah, I'll meet you down the station then. What time do you wanna go down?'

'I'll see you there at ten, then?'

'Ten in the morning?'

'Tidy. See you Saturday.'

'Bye J.' she swayed off and I had lust written across my forehead.

I practically wished the week away. I didn't tell my Mam about the date, I mean she hadn't told me every detail about her and Doctor Adulterer, so I wasn't going to mention one little thing about Kaleigh 'perfect' Adams. I did however tell Dad and mike who whooped with joy (well, Mike did) and kitted me out with some completely un-camp clobber to go to the city.

Friday night was the worst. When I was five or six, I had to be Joseph in the nativity play, I had to hold Hannah Evans's hand and sing some poxy carol, the night before I was sick all over Julie's table, next door. It could have been the two tins of Postman Pat spaghetti I'd eaten earlier in the night and the fact Davy and myself had been playing stuck in the bloody mud on full stomachs anyway, Mam told Julie that it must have been nerves. That is how my stomach felt the night before my first proper date and I hadn't eaten anything let alone two tins of novelty spaghetti.

Anyway, Saturday eventually turned up and I didn't get off to the best starts. Firstly, it was so bloody hot, the pale green polo shirt Mike had given me showed every part of sweat that formed a sort of film on my body. That's right, I had marks round my armpits, all down my back and under my man boobs too. I mean, I'm not even fat but I looked like I had serious issues. So, I changed. Then I'd run out of hair gel and as a quick, desperate attempts to salvage my look I used Mam's hair products. What a bloody mistake that was. My hair ended up smelling of bloody strawberries. Not exactly the manly rugby player scent I was hoping to present.

Then to top my stressful morning off when I turned up at the station, not only was Kaleigh there to greet me looking all sweet and perfect, but she was accompanied by several of her girls and Meeky, Wedgy and bloody Rassoul! Rassoul! The cheek of it.

'Alright Jonathan Jones, where you sneaking off to?' Meeky had that glint in his eye, the one which sparkled bloody trouble.

'Not sneaking Meeky, I is off to the city boy.'

'And whom you be off with, kid?' I hated it when he called me kid, he's bloody two months younger than me.

'He's coming with us.' nice one Kaleigh. I really wanted the 'one of the girls' image.

'As in; you lot?' the boys started laughing. I had to give it to Rassoul, sneaky bastard. A couple of weeks ago Meeky wanted to kill him, it's because of me he's even got friends.

'Don't play games Meek. You knew we were all meeting up today.' did she just say; 'we were all meant to meet'? Fucking hell this was a group outing. How come the boys hadn't said anything? Oh what a fucking set up.

The day itself didn't get much better either. When we got to Cardiff we all split up, as in boys went left, girls went right. So much for my proper bloody date. I honestly thought things couldn't get much bloody worse. That was until I heard Wedgy say;

'What she say then, Meek?'

'She hasn't text back yet.'

'Oooh.' Rassoul said. 'She is very pretty, yes?'

'What you on about, lads?' I couldn't keep the bitterness out of my voice.

'Meeky's only bloody texting Kaleigh.' Wedgy looked like he was about to combust with excitement. 'To see if she'll get her tits out.' I sweat to god, my heart stopped. I felt it pump, stop, pump, stop and then properly stop, like. What chance in hell did I have in winning Kaleigh over if I was up against Meeky for Christ sake. I may as well be trying to win bloody Angelina Jolie off Brad bloody Pitt!

It was definitely the sound of Meeky's brand spanking new mobile phone screaming that he had a text message that got my heart rate, not only going again but racing. Kaleigh was bound to want him not me, I mean, I was jack shit compared to Meeky. He was god of everything and I was the dude that cleaned his sandals.

'What she say then?' Wedgy was practically salivating at the thought of Kaleigh getting her boobs out and I know I had no right in taking the higher moral ground, seen's as I spend most nights dreaming about her lovely, perfect boobs, but seriously, how dare he treat her like a piece of meat. I was just about to give him a piece of my mind when Meeky said;

'Fuck up Wedge. It's got nothing to do with you.' and it was moments like these that I knew there must definitely be a god up there. There was this one time, we were down the club after a cup game and Meeky tried it on with this girl. She was about twenty one and mega smart. Blonde hair, blue eyes, typical chocolate girl mind, fit but she knew it. She knocked Meeky back about four counties and for the rest of the night Meeky wore this look on his face. A real pissed off expression. All the boys called it his 'reflection look' I instantly recognised the 'look'. Kaleigh had told him to piss off. And, seriously my shoulders felt three hundred times lighter than they had and my heart rate slowed back down to a normal pace. Back in the game. After about, what felt like fourteen hours of wandering around the city, Wedgy phoned the girls, who turned up with like a million shopping bags each and we all got on the train home. And indeed, it was the train home when things started to get interesting. Well, interesting for me anyway. We were half way up the valley when Kaleigh came to sit by me. And don't get me wrong I was really chuffed, not to mention all tingly and tense at the same time! I decided to play it cool, anyway, I mean, she'd led me to believe we were going on a proper date, hadn't she?

'Sorry, J.' she whispered which made several things flash through my head. One: she didn't want anyone to know we'd (as in me and her) arranged to sod off together. And, two: something illicit (hopefully) was about to be said?

'I couldn't stop the girls so I thought I'd better ask the boys, so it wouldn't be weird, for you like.' She smiled. 'So, you forgive me, right?' Time out! Her hand, her actual hand was rubbing my thigh, which felt really nice in jeans! So nice I felt my dick stir, the traitor we were meant to be playing hard to get.

'We all meeting down the club after then, its karaoke and we're bound to get served?' saved by the Wedgy, so to speak.

'Yeah, I'm up for that.' my voice was slightly high and I was a tad breathless. Christ, the girl must have know how she affected me. Jesus, she was still rubbing and smiling when the train pulled up at the station and I was not just hard I was rock solid. Which was quite a hard look (excuse the pun) to manoeuvre off the four, fifteen from Cardiff.

Shagging Kaleigh on the terraces was nothing like shagging that Claire/chicken thing. For a start, I wasn't steaming drunk or battered. It wasn't brilliant, but don't get me wrong her tits were well worth waiting for, pale and wobbly. Kaleigh herself tasted of blue WKD and I could tell she was dead nervous even though she had insinuated the whole thing.

I'll start at the beginning. We all met down the club at seven, like arranged, and as Wedgy predicted all the boys got served no problemo. So there I was, not intestinally mind, pumping the alchopops into Miss Adams. Now, I know it must seem like I was deliberately trying to get the poor girl pissed out of her head, but seriously I was just trying to come across generous, you know, good boyfriend material, like.

Anyway, we, as in me and all the boys, got up to sing 'We are the Champions' on karaoke and I was just feeling cidered up enough to possibly get up and sing a phonics solo when Jenna Brewer, Kaleigh's friend, told me to go out to the terraces because Kaleigh was waiting out there foe me. I know, I know, slightly playground behaviour but hell, at the end of the day I am fifteen!

Right, so I'm outside and I find Kaleigh quite high up on the terraces and even though she's swaying slightly and her eyes look like disco balls she still looks amazing. God, even being steaming suited her. She was wearing this red top that was sitting quite awkwardly on her at this point, with a white skirt that looked really good, even if it did have a couple of blue stains on it, because she's got really long, toned legs that were still brown from the summer.

'Jon.' she slurred. 'Come here, babe.'

'Ooh, someone's screwed.'

'No, I'm alright babe.' she then sort of wobbled a bit too far, so, me being the gentleman I am sort of, ran to catch her. It honestly wasn't a ploy to get her in my arms, cross my fingers.

'Thanks babe. I nearly went then, didn't I?'

'Yeah.' we were closer than close now, she had her arms round my neck and I had my leg in between her skirt so it only seemed polite to start snogging. Now, I know your probably thinking that there is no way on earth that I should have taken advantage or even considered shagging Kaleigh in this state, and seriously they were the last rational thoughts I had before I slipped a Durex on and lifted her skirt (I wasn't being cocky by carrying condoms round with me but, after my first sexual encounter I came away with little friends, didn't I? so it seemed a sensible idea to have a supply of the old rubbers in my wallet.).

So, as I said the sex itself was fumbly but strangely nice. Like, this time (don't laugh) I found myself whispering into Kaleigh's ear to make sure she was OK. It couldn't have been an incredibly comfy experience for her – on her back, on concrete, pissed, with my nearly eleven stone thrusting in and out of her.

We were half way through when Kaleigh decided to spring a lovely surprise on me, "You know it's my first time, don't you?" Holy shit, I'd taken her cherry, deflowered her. What the fuck was I playing at? I mean at least with the chicken the chances are I'd never ever see her again so even if my performance was utterly pathetic, she couldn't exactly dent my reputation because we didn't live in the same country let alone know the same people. But Kaleigh, well, she knew everyone I knew and if it was her first time she was probably expecting fireworks and rainbows and the Earth moving and stuff, because girls are like that, right?

'Is it your first time too?'

'Yeah.' now, I'd really done it. Why on Gods earth had I felt the need to tell that whooping bloody lie? I really wish I had a therapist sometimes. Someone that could dissect my behaviour because I couldn't work myself out, one little bit.

'Good.' she said and it must have been nerves because at that moment my eyes crossed and I came.

'Sorry.'

'That's OK. Are we done?'

'I'm so sorry, do you want me to carry on?'

'No, you're OK. I think my backs bleeding.' my spunk had remarkably sobered her up, so that was something at least. After we'd shrugged our clothing back to normal-ish positions and mumbled quite a few pleasantries;

'Sorry about the blood.'

'No problem, sorry for coming so quick.'

'That's OK. It was nice.'

'Sure?'

'Yeah.'

'Shall I walk you home?'

'yes please.'

Don't get me wrong the walk was slightly awkward, I mean, we had just had sex and not any type of sex, oh no, we'd had Kaleigh's first sex, ever! And yes, she had bled and yes of course it was all over her white skirt. I only hoped when we got to her Mam's that her parents were either out, in bed or pissed out of their heads. Because the state of Kaleigh would be quite difficult to explain. She didn't look like a rape victim or anything but she did look a little dazed, a little pissed and a little non-virginal and upset. Fuck, what was she upset for? Oh I hope I wasn't shit.

'No. you were fine it's just....' oh my god, I'd said that out loud. 'It's just, well it's gone now hasn't it?'

'Yeah, but if you want we can try it again. I'll be better next time, I promise.' she smiled up at me.

'It wasn't you, JJ. You were lovely. I just mean, that's it I'll never have it back. You must know what I mean, yours has gone too.' she giggled and I was so grateful it was dark and she couldn't see me blush.

Chapter Thirty-Four

As if taking the girl of my dreams virginity wasn't enough for one night, when I got home a hell of a lot more fun was awaiting for me to deal with.

I knew something was up the minute I saw the kitchen light on. I mean, by the time I'd slowly walked (to get my head round everything) back from Kaleigh's it had to have been past midnight, although I wasn't exactly in the frame of mind to note particulars, like the time. But the light on, struck me as odd because Mam had been hitting the hay relatively early the last couple of weeks.

Anyway, hooray for me Mam picked that particular Saturday to have a funny bloody turn. Apart from the kitchen light another clue, amazingly enough, that something was wrong, was the fact everything in the hall way had been tied up, like a mock spider web. And after I ambled through the first part of the assault course, true to Mam's psychotic form, everything in the living room, dining room, back bloody garden and all up the stairs was also tied up. It was the kitchen where the biggest surprise of all was waiting.

Amongst the string obstacles in nothing but his pants was Doctor Atwood.

'Hello Jonathan. How was your night?' how was my night? Was this fella for real? My mother, his fiancée had obviously had a wobbler and tied the poor bugger up, in his pants, in our kitchen.

'Are you alright?' I was too gob smacked to move.

'Yes. Fine thanks. Um … I'm not sure where your mother is.'

'Is she having an episode or is this some weird sex thing?'

'No, no she's not feeling too good.' well, that was something I suppose. Shit, what m must he be thinking? Poor sod had agreed to marry a bloody nut job. Let me refrain that poor sod had left his wife and kids to marry a bloody nut job. I started climbing towards him. I mean, it wasn't exactly dignifying sitting in someone's kitchen half naked, was it?

'She's been quite good recently, really. So I suppose a blip is expected, isn't it?' it felt weird asking a doctor in underwear about medical stuff. Not that it didn't feel weird talking about the weather and stuff either, its just we never quite got round to it!

'I think it's my fault.' he said. 'There were things I needed to tell her, things I should have said at the beginning of our relationship.'

'About your wife and kids?'

'Oh. So you know?'

'Yeah, my dinner lady told me.'

'Your dinner lady?'

'Marion.' God, Mam had obviously learnt to tie military bloody knots in the nut house.

'Oh, Marion. She's my…'

'Your mother in law. I know.' he looked at his feet and I felt mega sorry for him. I genuinely liked this bloke and I thought he'd be good for My Mam. Obviously, not good in the way that made her tie the house up with string like, but good.

I was mid un-doing the doc and counting to five hundred in my head to avoid the awkward atmosphere when the front door clicked and it sounded like a herd of elephants, singing elephants came in; *We're off to see the wizard, the wonderful wizard of Oz!'*

'What the' I left Doctor Atwood half undone and ventured out to the hallway where my Mam, crazy Nan and poor long suffering Bamp stood wearing horse riding hats, (god only knows where the hell they'd picked them up from.) those funny jodhpur things, big black riding boots (Bamp had green welly substitutes on.) and they were all carrying whips. Singing incredibly loudly, after midnight I might add.

'Hiya lovely, we're here for the show jumping event.' Crazy Nan was first to speak and looked pretty ecstatic. 'You got any gin?' Oh shit. One clinically crazy mother crossed with one half crazy Nan equals one very messy Saturday night.

'Do you like my arena, babe?' Mam's eyes were glassy – always a bad sign. 'Come in here, kids, the main events in the kitchen?' oh shit, was she having an episode or was she just mad, as in very angry with the doctor?

'Mam, maybe you should take Nan and Bamp, Hi Bamp.'

'Hi Jon.' he looked tired and a bit pissed.

'…through to the living room and I'll bring you drinks through?' Mam looked at me like I was from another planet, a look I'd seen before, right before she tried to

123

bloody stab me. Shit. There was a tense silence although to be fair I was the only one who picked up on it.

'No babe. Let your Nan through to see…um, what's-his-name?'

'Doctor Atwood, Mam.'

'That's the bugger. Yeah, come and see him, kids.' they traipsed past me. I felt so sorry for Doctor A, I mean, OK he'd obviously been a bit of a shit, but seriously he didn't deserve this treatment.

Nan cracked up instantly. Of course, if you were steaming and probably dosed up on Valium this type of situation would be a scream, wouldn't it?

I'd watched this documentary once about human sacrifice and the scene in my kitchen the night I took Kaleigh Adam's virginity, showed an incredible resemblance to that programme. Mam and Nan just stood cackling while Bamp had plonked himself on a kitchen stool and just snored his way through the ordeal.

'Shouldn't we let Doctor Atwood get up now, Mam?'

'Why babes?' God, at fifteen how the hell was I meant to take on a bloody parental role, voice of reason, fucking judge/police man?

'Well, he's probably a bit uncomfortable now, aren't you?' it wouldn't have surprised me at this point if Doctor A had shit himself. The poor fella had a look of pure terror across his face and his voice quivered as he answered me.

'I could do with using the toilet, if that's OK?'

'Of course it is, right Mam?' I willed my Mam to just say yes and let the poor bugger go. I'm sure this situation could definitely get Mam locked up, whether that be locked up in an institute or locked up in a bloody prison.

'Um…' Mam looked confused and as she seemed to take the whole scene in, it was if she snapped out of whatever zone she'd been in.

'I'm not feeling too good, J.' Mam looked about twelve years old. 'I think I may need a lie down.'

'Before you go to bed, love, I'm feeling a bit fruity, have you got any Pina Colada stuff here?'

'I'll get some now Nan, Can you just untie the Doctor while I put Mam to bed?'

Once Mam was safely sedated and in the confinements of her bedroom I took on the role of responsible adult in the war zone, informally known as the arena, formally known as the kitchen.

It took me approximately twenty minutes to free Doctor A, fair play to Mam she hadn't messed about with the knots. It took a further hour and half to untie the rest of the house. Nan was completely wasted and Bamp had remained in the same position through out.

'Is he OK?' Doctor Atwood was now fully clothed and drinking some very strong tea, apparently it's good for shock.

'Who?' Nan made an attempt to swivel her head but the gin got the better of her logic so she only managed to move her clouded eyes.

'He's on about Bamp, Nan.'

'Oh him. He'll be fine. Cant handle his beer, that one.' Nan started hooting but Doctor Atwood's face took on a some what professional expression. He started feeling Bamp's wrists and neck and put his face really close to Bamp's head. 'Shit.' He mumbled. Which was probably the most un-appropriate word he'd ever said, ever.

'He's dead.' oh, for fucks sake, seriously, this couldn't be happening to me. First, I practically stole Kaleigh's virginity then I came home to find My Mam's fiancée tied up to the max in his pants and now my grandfather had snuffed it! If I don't need therapy by the time I'm twenty one then it'll be a bloody miracle.

'He can't be dead he hasn't finished his lager yet, and we've got a party to go to tomorrow up the cricket club. He can't be dead.' Nan carried on sipping her gin as if Doctors made these type of startling statements quite frequently.

'Nan!'

'Calm down, lurvy. Your Bamp's a very heavy sleeper. Just give him a big nudge.'

'I'm sorry. He really is dead. Jon, can you get me the phone please.' at this point I was contemplating asking Doctor Atwood if he fancied joint counselling.

'Oh I knew he'd bloody die tonight, I just knew it. I woke up this morning, or was it this afternoon after my nap? Anyway, I thought, I bet he's going to die today.' it was this sentence that helped me realise that maybe Mam's illness was genetic. Nan was tapped. She's got to be the only person I know, in the world, who takes the news of her husband's death as a bloody in-convenience. "Said he'd take me to Benidorm next year to, the bugger, now he's gone and bloody died." She poured herself another drink and the look on Doctor Atwood's face was priceless.

'What do we do now then?' she asked. 'JJ, have you got any lemon by any chance?' shit, was this shock? I put my head quite far in the fridge, to not only look for lemon but to cool my head and to avoid looking at the corpse that used to be my grandfather. Jesus Christ.

'How am I going to get home now?' she had to have been in shock, surely not even Nan was that blatant? 'I'll have to get a taxi, I don't fancy staying here. Your Mam doesn't get the sheets soft enough for my liking.'

'Why don't you have a cup of tea Mrs...?'

'Jones. And no thank you, I'm quite happy with my gin, dear.' and that was that, basically. We sort of tip-toed round the fact Bamp was dead on a kitchen stool and that Nan refused to react to this fact and the ordeal of the whole evening until the ambulance turned up. When we continued to tip-toe around the fact the ambulance had taken Bamp away, that Nan still hadn't seemed to hit reality (or soberness) and that Mam was still sedated upstairs. Jesus Christ - only me.

'Well, I'd better be off. I think I've had as much as I can take for one day.' God, the Doctor had aged about seventy five years. And the poor bastard had signed up to be involved with us lot by putting a diamond on Mam's finger. Bet he wished he'd never done that now.

'Ooh, do you think you could give me a lift please? I'll get out by the Red Lion if it's easier.' God, the woman was insatiable, she'd just lost her husband and she was all ready thinking about pubs.

'I'll take you to your front door, Mrs Jones.' Doctor Atwood was a bloody good egg. I hoped him and Mam could sort everything out. Well, I hoped he hadn't been scarred for life and could find away round all this madness to stick it out with my Mam.

'Well, that's that then. Thanks for the gin JJ. Tell your Mam I'll give her a call tomorrow.' and bright as a button Nan skipped (not literally, mind) out of the front door behind Doctor Atwood.

Fucking hell. What a bloody day.

Chapter Thirty-Five

Don't get me wrong, I'm no expert on funerals or anything, but you really can't beat a valley bash. The week leading up to the 'big day' as Nan had labelled it, went by as a bit of a blur. To be honest Nan was excited for the wake because of the massive piss up that was guaranteed after the ceremony. (I mean, she could get drunk without being judged for it.) Not so much for the burning of her husband, although you never quite know.

Anyway, my grandfather had suffered a massive heart attack and apparently he wouldn't have felt a thing, so that was something at least. There was one good thing about my grandfather passing away, was the fact I was allowed to bunk off school for the week and therefore did not have to face bloody Kaleigh Adams since I'd de-flowered the bugger. And I was sure by the time I finally went back to school someone would have participated in a far bigger scandal therefore taking a vast amount of attention (unwanted I may add) off yours truly. Also, my Mam had a pretty good week too. Obviously we didn't mention the tying-the-doctor-up-incident but she properly took her medication and we had a relatively stable seven days. Thank God. And, I knew I knew things were running far too smoothly because; let's face it, it's me. But, I really didn't want to give in to the niggling feeling of anticipation.

Well, the fun started when the family car turned up outside Nan's. Nan was pretty steaming as soon as Mam and myself turned up just before eight, in the morning mind. Now, in normal circumstances, the widow, being pissed before the ceremony would have been slightly odd, but the fact it was my Nan and if she had been sober, would have been abnormal. But seriously she was proper wrecked. Slurring and stumbling like a good one.

'Love, how many have you had?' Mam asked and as I glanced at her you could tell she was feeling better because she had those lines across her face that showed she was concerned.

'Not nearly enough, luvvy.' oh hell! Dad and Mike turned up about half hour before we had to leave for the church and seriously – what a bloody pair, they were like the bastard odd couple for Christ sake.

Mike looked like something out of a cheap Mafia film. The best way to describe what he looked like would be to say he was the image of an angry little Italian.

'Oh babes, I can't get over it, you look fab sweetie.' he dabbed his eyes for affect as he gushed over my Nan. Dad, on the other hand looked quite rough, which was not really surprising since he'd just lost his father. He looked old. And I don't think I'll ever forget the look of sadness he wore that morning, before the put on his brave face that was. Pure sadness. Mind you, he wasn't that sad that he hadn't kitted himself out in head to probably toe with tip top gear. For an oldish gay man he just looked, well... GAY!

'You alright, J?' shit I must have been staring.

'Yeah. I'm OK Dad.' he gave me a weak smile.

'Babes, you're looking hot too. No offence but death is really becoming for this family.'

'MIKE!' everyone bar Nan shouted. And then we all sort of giggled, you had to give it to Mike he knew how to break tension. And he'd made Mam feel loads better, because before the 'hot' comment she'd spent, like a million hours saying how frumpy she looked.

Now, I don't want to sound all weird and stuff, but to be honest I flew past normality ages ago, didn't I? Anyway, being in the big black car made me feel special. Loads of old blokes took their hats and stuff off as we passed them, which was mad. Nan whipped her hip flask out about half way to church and pretty soon after everyone had had a swig of Sambuca (Yes, Nan will drink anything at a push.) the conversation got sentimental. Which was nice because I'd been expecting the whole day to be sad, sad and sadder. But, hey how wrong could I have been?

'Remember when he pissed in his hat?' Nan's eyes were crystal clear and her tone was warm, you could tell the fondness she'd felt for Bamp. 'We were on a trip with the club and the silly bugger got drunk on the bus on the way to Tenby, I think it was Tenby anyway.'

'Doesn't sound like Dad, does it?' Dad was beaming.

'Oh it was. He was so drunk he took his hat off and pissed in it, at the side of the motorway.'

'Mam. Wasn't that Dave the drunk from up the Tump who did that?' Dad was nodding.

'Was it now? Well, bugger me.' everyone laughed.

'You're father was pissed on that trip, mind.' now, I wouldn't have said I was a psychologist or whatever they bloody are, but I felt the mood change, though I wasn't sure why... and then... my Nan came out with it; "That was the trip I caught him shagging about.' I'm not moralistic or anything but seriously old people should never, ever use words such as 'shagging'.

'Mam should you be going into all this today, I mean it's…!'

'Let her get it off her chest, babes.' Mike's eyes were like saucers.

'Mike! Don't be so fucking nosy for once in your life.' Dad looked and sounded pretty mad. "Let's leave it there for today, is it?" Mike looked like a wounded I-Ti.

'No, it's OK. It's probably time to let it all out, anyway.' Nan sounded the most sober I'd heard her all week, although her hands and lips were quivering. "It was only the once I caught him."

'Oh shit.' Dad put his face in his hands.

'And it was up in Tenby. He was pissed to.' She giggled, which was a bit freaky to be honest. My stomach sunk a little lower as the thought of Nan and Bamp swinging processed through my mind. 'We'd all been on the drink all day, like so when I walked into our hotel room and seen him… well, I just thought; it can't be, obviously I'm far more drunk than I thought.' you could have seriously have dropped a pin at this point, I swear. 'Love' he said. 'Its not what it looks like.' But, it was of course.'

'Why are you saying this, today of all days Mam?'

'Because I've already kept it in to long as it is. You see, he was with…he was with, another man.'

For fucks sake! Why doesn't someone hot the double whammy now and say; 'actually J, you were adopted at birth!' Jesus, could this family dig up anymore dirt?

'Mam?' Dad looked gob smacked.

'Of course he was mortified after and swore to me it was only the once. And, to be honest, I drunk through it all.' Nan proceeded to cackle for about ten minutes solid. Mike looked like he was about to laugh or cry, I'm not sure. Mam just looked, well, like she'd just seen Bamp tap the window from the hearse in front and wave and Dad looked like he was about to snuff it himself.

'For fucks sake.' Dad's tears started. 'Why today Mam?' Mike rubbed his leg and my stomach flipped.

Fucking hell what if this gay thing really was genetic? I had that hot saliva stuff that sort of invades your mouth just before you throw up. Suddenly the car was boiling hot and sweat trickled my palms and my face. Shit! But I'd shagged two girls so I couldn't be gay, could I? If you're gay do you still get stiffies? Holy fuck! Everything started to swirl in front of my eyes and it was if everyone was in slow motion. Oh my god, seriously what if I'm gay?

Splash.

'Jon. Oh baby are you OK?' the sun was glaring into my eyes and everyone was peering over me and I could tell I was lying on a very, very hard floor because my back was in bastard agony.

'Jon, how many fingers am I holding up?' Mam was waving her hand in front of my eyes.

'Jesus.' I whispered.

'Oh my god he's with the lord.' Nan put herself in the prayer position. 'Please lord, take care of our boy.'

'Mam, for Christ sake, give it a rest he's just a bit dazed.'

'Jon, Jon, CAN. YOU. SEE. ME?'

'I'm sure he's not deaf, babe.' Mike looked bored. 'He'll be OK now it's probably just too much for him.'

'You sure it's not just too much for you? For fucks sake Mike the boys just passed out, it's kind of serious.' Dad's tone was slightly nasty and although I couldn't see I imagined Mike to have his wounded puppy expression neatly in place under his designer sunglasses. Fair play there's nothing quite like a funeral to stir things up.

'I'm OK.' my voice sounded miles away. I started to get up from…well, wherever the hell I was lying.

'You sure doll? Shall we get you an ambulance?' ha ha! Was Mam nutty again, or did she really think I was in need of medical assistance?

'No, I'm fine. Urgh.' my head spun and I felt sick. So, this is what its like to pass out!

'Careful love.' there was an awkward silence whilst everyone looked concerned and stared.

'I'm OK.'

'I hate to trouble you, um, but we're sort of holding things up and well, these things run on quite a tight schedule.' it was the limo driver. Oh good, I hadn't missed the funeral, had I? I had a really uneasy feeling, like I'd forgotten an appointment or something really important. You know when you're meant to be worrying about something but then something else makes you forget about the something you're supposed to be worrying about and then you worry about the worrying? Well, that's how I was feeling as I came round as they ushered me back into the limo.

And of course it wasn't until well after the service and the crematorium and it wasn't until the fourth or even fifth cider slid down my throat at the wake did I remember what I was meant to be worrying about.

And boy did it hit me good. Was the gay gene actually in our family? Was I gay? Oh hell, my collar did that thing, yet again where it suddenly was way, way, too tight for my neck.

Of course, this time I really considered the possibility that I may be a homosexual. Bugger that little niggle at the back of my brain, I had to really think hard which resulted in a panic attack.

I never realised why they called them panic attacks that was until I had a bugger. I can't really put it into word how I felt in the cubicle of the men's at the club. But I hope to god I never, ever have another one again. I had all these mad things going round my head and I couldn't breathe, like seriously couldn't breathe it was horrible. I couldn't be gay – I really did fancy women and I'd had sex with two! But what if it was in my genetic make up? I mean, Dad had a bloody wife and son before he realised he was one and look at Bamp for Christ sake? Shit, I was considering the easiest form of suicide or hibernation at least, when;

'JJ, you in here?' Mike. Top bender.

'Yeah. I'm here.' Can't breathe, Can't breathe.

'You OK, babe. Sorry, buddy?' I could even hear him checking his reflection.

'Um, not really.'

'What's up?' I wasn't entirely comfortable with discussing these type of issues with Mike in a men's toilet to be brutally honest but considering my lack of oxygen issue I didn't think I really had a choice in the matter.

'JJ, you look bloody terrible. What the hell is it?' it had taken most of my strength to simply open the toilet door.

'I… don't…know…Well, I do.' I rubbed my chest and hung for dear life of the sinks whilst Mike faffed around mumbling about ambulances and parents. 'Mike, do you think I'm gay?' it just came out, I couldn't hold it back, I had to know, and Mike seemed like an expert if ever I met one.

'Is this why you're having some sort of episode?' he then started laughing. 'Sorry sweetie. Calm down your not gay, you really wouldn't have to ask if you were.'

'Yeah, but what if it's in my genes, like Dad and…'

'There is NO such thing J. honestly, you're not gay.' it took a while but slowly relief started to seep through my muscles and my shoulders lowered. My breathing pattern was still fast but a hell of a lot easier. Mike was right, I wasn't gay, I fancied girls and proper womanly girls with hips and tits not these tiny short haired boyish ones either. I was definitely not a BENDER! And then my thoughts went down another track; even if I was gay, was it such a big problem? Life was too short for this bollocks surely. As long as I was happy, ey? And, now I was sure I was straight I could take the risk and give Mike a manly hug.

I hadn't heard the door click.

I spent all that day at Kaleigh's. She made me scrambled eggs and toast and we watched MTV all day. Mam was quite angry when I phoned apparently I hadn't told anyone where I was going the night before. God, she would have been really mad if she'd known I'd spent the night with a girl and she'd probably go berserk if she found out I'd spent the day (a school day, I might add) having blow jobs off one.

'I'll be home for tea!' I told her as I clicked my mobile phone shut, playing angry son role, although if I'm brutally honest I never ever wanted to leave Kaleigh's. I hadn't been this happy for bloody ages. When I was with her, even though I was still a little bit paranoid whether she liked me or not or whether I'd said the right thing and stuff, but I felt like we were in a little bubble and we were safe from the whole school, whole valley, whole bloody world in fact. She made me feel like a normal teenage boy not JJ with the gay Dad and basket case Mam but JJ normal fifteen year old rugby player stud.

Obviously I knew this beautiful feeling wouldn't last because this is me, but for the moment I was I was glad to enjoy feeling this way. And fair play it lasted a couple of weeks. I was introduced to Kaleigh's parents as her bloke and be-grudgingly I introduced her to Mam (on one of her good days) and then Dad and Mike, meetings that both went really well. Even the boys at school were dead pleased OK I did get some playful stick as opposed to angry, nasty, violent stick.

And then it happened. It all went tits up like I'd expected. Like, I had been waiting for it to. It was Friday afternoon and as the bell went for the end of the day I rushed to the school main gates to meet Kaleigh, liked I'd been doing every day for the last couple of weeks. I loved the end of the day usually, like I loved the beginning when I walked Kaleigh to school, like I loved morning and afternoon breaks when I'd meet Kaleigh, like I loved dinner times when I'd meet Kaleigh and we'd have lunch and hold hands and snog. So, basically I was loving every second of every minute I got to spend with my amazing girlfriend, the spectacular Kaleigh bloody Adams.

I still couldn't believe that she was mine, out of everyone in school, everyone in Wales even she had picked me. I mean, seriously she could have had anyone. And then that bloody Friday turned up and everything went horribly wrong.

I'd waited at the gates for like ten minutes and I'd started to get a bit worried because Kaleigh is hardly ever late, she was late once but that was because she'd had to go to the pan first, and anyway, she'd text me to let me know. So, ten minutes turned into fifteen and before I knew it I had been waiting a whole half hour.

'Where are you?' my voice must have sounded quite harsh down the mobile but seriously I'd worked myself up into a full blown panic.

'Um...J, it's Jenna, Kaleigh doesn't want to speak to you.' I could hear the words 'fucking' and 'prick' and 'arse-hole' in the background.

'Why what have I done? Please put Kaleigh on.'

'Seriously J, I'd leave her alone for a bit.' and the phone went dead. What the fuck had I done? We were fine yesterday; we'd had sex behind the post office. Oh hell, what if she was pregnant or worse what if I'd been so shit she couldn't even stomach being near me?

I spent the walk home debating all possibilities from Kaleigh fancying someone else to maybe she'd had some shit about my Dad or even my Mam? It was just as I got to my front door when my phone beeped.

ONE TEXT MESSAGE RECIVED
FROM KALEIGH
LIAR!!!!

Oh shit! Oh shit! Oh fucking shit! The chicken! It had to be the chicken up in Blackpool, it had to be the whooping great big mother fucking lie I told about my virginity. And of course it had come right back round to bite me on my big fat gutless arse.

And, as if things couldn't get any worse when I got into the kitchen I found my Mam making tin towers with all the contents of our cupboards.

'Mam, what the hell are you doing now?' she had a bobble hat on and some swimming goggles, inflatable arm bands and green Wellies, she used to walk our dog in.

'Hi honey, no Kaleigh?' Ouch! 'Doctor Atwood's coming round for his tea later, if you don't mind that is? Anyway, thought I'd keep busy until I have to get ready.'

'But why are you dressed like that, for Christ sake?' I know I sounded harsh but I really had, had an absolute guts-full. My anger was bubbling, I could almost feel it tickling my patience, teasing me to scream and smash things up. Mam looked a bit wounded; 'I'm alright J, just fancied a bit of harmless fun.'

'In arm bands and goggles?' again, my tone was angry, probably cause I was, but seriously when was I gonna get a bloody break?

'Yes Jonathan, in bloody arm bands and goggles and to be honest if I wanted to wear a bloody rabbit suit it's got nothing to do with you. I'm bored J, bored shitless and up to my eyes in poxy medication so, lay off me.'

Now it was my turn to look upset. I was one selfish boy, so wrapped up in why everyone and everything was out to get me I'd forgotten that other people have a hell of a lot more going on to deal with.

'I'm sorry, I've had a bad day, I wasn't thinking. I'll be in my room.'

'Do you want something to eat?'

'No thanks, I'll see you in a bit.' and with that I went to my room to wallow.

Chapter Thirty-Seven

If I had counted, which I didn't by the way, but if I had counted I had probably checked my mobile about thirty thousand times in the two and a half hours I had been wallowing. My moods had gone from sulking to angry to sentimental to angry to pathetic to angry back to sulking then straight back to angry once again. I also battled with the debate of whether to text Kaleigh, ring Kaleigh or ignore Kaleigh completely? Oh to be young.

How the hell had she found out about the chicken? Maybe my little friends had not cleared up and escaped through the condom into her... her, whatever the correct name for a fanny is. Or maybe, one of the boys had told her? It had to have been Meeky he was jealous of me and her from the beginning? Oh god, yet again what a bloody mess.

At about eight o clock I heard the front door click and Mam's voice gushed through the floor boards and then Doctor Atwood's awkward grumble crawl up the stairs. God, even my parents, if not weird ones, had better love lives than me. I decided to go pay my old Man a visit, I mean he was pretty useless in the girl department but Mike was pretty clued up on the whole female thinking strategies. And, OK the thought of discussing these issues was a bit freaky, at the end of the day he offered pretty good advice, and it wasn't as if I had butties queuing up, was it?

Leaving, I popped my head around the kitchen door to let Mam know where I was going, in hindsight, (new word) I wish I hadn't bothered.

Thank god Mam had changed into some sort of red ensemble thing but not thanking god for letting me witness the sight before me. She was sort of straddling Doctor Atwood on the breakfast bar, snogging like, well, teenagers. "I'm off to Dad's." they didn't even look up so me being the dutiful son let them get on with it.

Mike and Dad were watching some sort of documentary on Sky with a bottle of wine at their feet when I walked in. I'd stopped knocking the door after we'd all bonded; they had after all told me to treat their house like my own.

'Hi son, this is a nice surprise. Want something to eat?' what was with everyone offering me grub, perhaps I'd lost weight?

'No thanks. Just come for a chat and stuff.' Mike looked like he was about to combust with happiness at the prospect of a 'gossip' as he called it. He manoeuvred himself so he was sort of hanging over the edge of sofa. 'What's happened? Is it your Mam.' he gasped; 'On no its Kaleigh isn't it?'

'Bloody women.' I sat deep into the arm chair and Dad got up and passed me a bottle of beer, I liked the way he treated me like a real bloke.

'Only one, mind.' well, sort of like a real bloke.

'Spill JJ, tell Mike all.'

'I've been a cock.' I sort of spat as I swallowed the way too fizzy lager. 'I told a massive lie.'

Dad and Mike oohed and aahed as I painfully re-told how I managed to lose my virginity to a bloody chicken and then in very brief detail how the lie had easily slipped out whilst we were, well while we were doing the deed.

'You're a little minx Jonathan Jones.' Mike looked quite proud. 'Quite the little, or not so little ladies man. You been bulking yourself up, boy?'

We spent the night dissecting the mess that had become my life. Weighing up the best plan of attack to win my woman back! Mikes ideas ranged from a simple bunch of flowers with a 'sorry' note to a bloody limo or bloody hot air balloon.

'I think honesty is probably the best policy with this one, Kid.' and I knew Dad was right of course I had to come clean and hope Kaleigh would be calm enough to just let me explain.

The weekend was pure hell. Kaleigh refused to answer her phone, she wouldn't even reply to my texts for Christ sake. I was literally going out of my bloody mind. You know when you see those mental people on TV, the ones worse than my Mam, in films and stuff where they just pace round rooms and rock in chairs well, that was what I'd become. She was driving me crazy, I just needed to explain myself.

I was halfway between getting angry and upset when Wedgy phoned me.

'We're gonna have a few cans round here if you fancy it? My Mam's away and Dad said he'd get us a crate.' I didn't exactly have any better offers, did I? Plus I was on the verge of a nervous breakdown. So, I had a cheese sandwich a shower and made my way for a day with the boys, if anything could cheer me up it would be a cider day with my buddies, or so I thought.

The day started quite well, we watched a pile of rugby league on the sports channels and slammed the cans into us. I was just beginning to relax and (nearly) forget about Kaleigh and her hatred for me when she cropped up in conversation.

'So, J how's married life?' this was clearly a dig, because if you (as in me) hadn't been spending much time with 'the lads' they get a bit touchy especially about girlfriends and so on. Mam said it was jealousy, I just thought they enjoyed ripping the piss into me.

'Not too good boys, in fact I think I may have been dumped.' it wasn't meant to sound light hearted it was just, I didn't have anything to lose and I was a little intoxicated and again, on the edge of being sentimental so being dumped wasn't seeming that bad really.

'I did hear.' Meeky was smirking and my light heartedness seemed to evaporate instantly.

'What did you ask for then?' I felt my muscles tightening and my heart pumping and without meaning to I had crushed my can in my hand and dribbles of cider was in between my fingers.

'Well, you know, just wanted to make sure my facts were right.' God, I could have wiped his smile clean off his smug, patronising bloody face. What was his problem?

'Well, now…you know.' I'd always thought the expression; you could cut the atmosphere with a knife, to be a stupid sentence and slightly impossible up until this point in my life. The air was thick with hostility and I felt everyone's heads spinning between me and the prick.

Thank god Wedgy chose that moment to ask; 'Anyone like some wine?' and everyone laughed at the ludicrous notion that Wedgy could even open a bloody bottle of wine. Everyone had a good old chuckle accept me and Meeky, we were to busy having some sort of weird stare off.

'I think I've had enough, boys.' the way I looked at it was it was best I leave before our friendship was tested, yet again. And really, before I made a first class twat of myself. As the air outside hit me so did the fury. How fucking dare he. What a wanker it had to have been him who told Kaleigh about that fucking chicken, that fucking worse mistake of my life. I wobbled a little bit as I made my way down Wedgy's posh drive. God, I was mad I was madder than bloody mad I was fuming and then for some crazy reason I thought it would be a good idea to go and see Kaleigh, have it out with her properly. Mohamed went to the mountain didn't he? Or whatever the stupid saying was. I was gonna tell her, well, I'd cross that bridge when I came to it but something needed to be said.

All the lights in Kaleigh's were off. Isn't it funny how when you've had a drink you lose all concept of time. I tried ringing her phone but it just kept going straight to voice mail.

'Kaleigh' why I thought whispering her name to a dark house would help was beyond me but I had a go anyway. 'Kaleigh…Kaleigh…Kaleigh!' an upstairs light came on. Curtains twitched. Kaleigh appeared. I was like a bloody rabbit caught in the headlights. All my Dutch courage had sobered up and legged it to the nearest pub for a sharp double. She was angry, her face looked hard and annoyed and the only thing I could think to do was sing. So I sang. At first it was just awkward words but after realising I had bugger all to lose I belted out Whitney Houston's, the greatest love. (Don't ask me how I knew the words…probably something to do with Mam, or come to think of it, more likely Dad.) Kaleigh's face looked slightly softer and she made her way downstairs and outside where, at this point, I was on her lawn giving the song my heart and soul.

'Jon, get up and stop.' not quite the reaction I was hoping for, but at least it was a form of conversation. I would even go as far to be cocky and say it was progress.

'Well, you came down.' she looked angry again. 'Kaleigh, give me a chance, let me explain, I'm really sorry I shouldn't have lied, it was just, well, that girl meant nothing, it was a drunken fumble, a Blackpool thing, she was minging and I didn't class it as special, not like me and you.'

'What are you talking about?'

'Me and that chicken from Blackpool. The one I, you know, lost my virginity to.'

'I, I have no idea what your talking about. J, I'm pissed off because you lied to me.'

'Yeah, about me losing my virginity to you?'

'No.' oh shit, oh crap, oh fuck. What have I done? 'No. you lied to me about me being invited to the wedding, I seen Mike in Tesco and he had no idea I was coming because they haven't even sent invites yet! I felt like an idiot banging on about my new bloody dress.' bollocks. 'But hey, thanks for clearing up the virginity thing you arse hole.' she was half shouting/ half crying. 'Just stay away from me J, just stay well clear you dick head.'

And that was that, that was how me and Kaleigh Adams officially split up. I was nothing but a super size cock of an idiot. If only I'd fucking asked what her problem was.

Sunday was somewhat sombre as I dealt with a horrible hangover and the fact I was nothing but a prick, over one of Nan's roasts. I usually liked Nan's Sunday dinners; she did better gravy than Mam. But, this particular Sunday even the Yorkshire puddings (Which she bought in a packet and only had to de-frost.) were too much for our stomach to bear.

'Would you like a sherry, J? It'll calm your shaking, boy. I had one this morning and I'm not shaking now.'

'Won't it make me worse, Nan?'

'No! What'll kill you will cure you. You've got a lot to learn my boy.'

Three and a half cooking Sherries later I found myself giggling with Nan explaining the hilariousness of nine and Kaleigh's argument. Obviously, I missed out anything that included sex, I wasn't that drunk.

'Oh what a shame.' Nan laughed, wiping her streaming eyes. 'I'm, sure it'll all work out alright though, love. These things have a way of working themselves out.'

'I hope so Nan, I really hope so.'

Chapter Thirty-Eight

The next day in registration, with yet another hell of a hangover, I heard the whispering before the blatant accusations surfaced. 'Gay', 'bender', 'up-the-arse', were just some of the phrases I picked up through the cloudiness of Nan's sherry headache. And, I'll be honest I didn't initially think the insults were directly aimed at me. I mean, in one week I'd been dumped, lost a friend, again, and got pissed…twice! It had been a busy couple of days literally, it was only when Darren Jones, AKA school dickhead came straight out and asked me who my 'partner' was, and yes he did that bloody irritating speech mark gesture with his bloody irritating hands, did I realise that the whispering and giggling was about yours truly.

'My partner?' I asked. (Stage sigh) hadn't I been through this all ready?

'Yeah. You've got a boyfriend now, haven't you?' I wasn't impressed with his pronunciation of boy-friend.

'Who've you heard that off?'

'Its all round school, everyone's talking about it.' I couldn't be sure, but I'm pretty positive Darren was fluttering his eyelashes at me.

'Jesus,' I mumbled. 'I'm not gay, I don't have a partner. I fancy bloody girls!' my head was pounding, I'd started sweating and I had effin' double maths next lesson so; to say I wasn't in the mood was one massive understatement.

'Well, SOR-RY! But, apparently someone seen you necking some Italian in the rugby club toilets a couple of weeks ago and now Kaleigh's finished with you because your well, gay.'

'Darren, that's the biggest, fattest...' Oh shit, the toilet... 'Lie. It's a lie, OK?'

'Alright buddy, take a chill pill.' and with that Darren Jones sort of shimmied off down the corridor whilst I re-lived mine and Mikes now; not so manly embrace in the gents.

By lunch time my life had become unbearable, again. I mean, seriously how much more bloody torture was I expected to go through. As if double maths wasn't bad enough, double maths sat on your tod was a living version of hell, but double maths on your tod with every member of your class making snide remarks and giggling must have actually been hell.

I decided not even to brave the outskirts of the canteen and I knew the chippy would be a minefield of insults, so I spent dinner time with my head in my hands in a changing room cubicle in the P.E department. I wasn't hungry even the thought of passing food through my mouth made me queasy and for some reason strangely sweaty.

And, it was in those changing rooms, the day of the hang over and rumours and general absolute bollocks, that I received my second glorious beating by, (another drum roll please) my wonderful fucking friends.

I hadn't been in there very long. I'd only briefly contemplated how crap everything was when I heard the door go and the pitter-patter of designer trainers on the hard concrete floor. I knew instantly it was my lot because trainers in school hours were a big no, no! So to be ultimately cool all my boys changed their Ted Baker school shoes at dinner and break time for their Nike pumps – only for the breaks mind.

It was Rassoul's whispering that came first and then Meeky's fist meeting poor Rassoul's arm, then he hissed at him to sssshhh.

'J, you in here mate?' now, if I'd been logical I would have stayed put, lowered my breathing and waited for the boys to piss off somewhere else. Of course, by now you've probably noticed, I don't have a single logical bone in my entire body.

Now, I'm not saying I bounded out all smiles and waves, but I really wasn't prepared for a bloody pasting.

'Alright lads?' I think it was Rassoul who threw the first punch which obviously stumped me straight away; I mean I really had had a tit full of that boy. Cheeky fucker indeed.

Anyway, I didn't even have time for the pain to register before another first landed in my face and another until I was on the floor receiving various trainers in my side, my head, my back. I'm sure you've got the picture by now.

I could briefly make out the words 'dirty' and 'liar' and some explicit descriptions of arse taking and receiving; blah, blah,blah details hadn't really been my priority. Luckily, or not so luckily they didn't leave me quite in the state they had last time but I was still pretty messed up. As I lay there on the cold floor with warm blood seeping from… well, I'm not sure where from, I was thinking how it wouldn't be a bad thing if I just died, right, there on the changing room floor.

I'm not sure how long I lay there for, it wasn't too long, I don't think, I mean no classes interrupted my bleeding session, so it could have been mere minutes or possibly a couple of hours. Everything was very hazy, they'd done a good job on my head this time, and I'd give them credit for that.

My head was pounding, spinning and cloudy all at the same time. I was having real difficulty focusing, the changing rooms had become a blurry screen, tainted pink as I groped around to get some sort of perspective.

'Oh my god.' I could make out a dazzling pair of trainers coming towards me. 'Can you hear me Jonathan?' it was Mrs Richards, our P.E teacher. And yes I could hear her perfectly I just couldn't reply – that was a whole different ball game. 'Jon, its OK, I'm going to get help.'

After being stitched and dosed in pain killers at A and E, I was on first name terms with the staff now. Dad had come down to collect me and this is where the interrogation started. Dad wanted answers, the police had been phoned and they wanted answers, my headmaster wanted answers and at one point I think the bloody cleaner wanted answers. Which was mad, because at no point did anyone consider the fact that maybe I would have liked answers.

I decided; for better or worse, to keep my mouth shut. I'd wait for my head to stop hurting and really consider my game plan. I knew immediately I didn't want the police involved, I mean I was no grass and even if the bastards had broken my nose again, the pigs would guarantee a bloody broken jaw, too.

Keeping Dad in the dark was a little harder. He was throwing the questions at me from all directions on the way home.

'Who, what, why?' it was all too much for Christ sake.

'Dad, can we leave this for today? My heads killing I watched his knuckles drain of all colour as he gripped the steering wheel of his new, highly impressive Nissan convertible. He bit his lip, I imagined if his teeth hadn't blocked it, the pile of abuse that must be loitering on his tongue desperate to be relived.

'I'm sorry, son. It's just …' he sighed, and it seemed to help his anger level. 'I can't believe this has happened again.'

'It's OK.' of course it wasn't. I felt like pure shit straight from a dogs arse. No, I felt like pure shit in between two pieces of mouldy bread. It was so wrong on so many levels it didn't feel real. 'Can I stay with you tonight, if you don't mind?'

'Of course you can.' we drove the rest of the way home in silence. Where the fuck was I going to get answers from this time? Why the hell had they given me another hiding? I was definitely going to have to get myself a brand new set of friends that was for sure. My nose felt enormous and my eyes like piss holes in the snow. My body was bruised but not broken this time, thank god. Jesus, what a mess. I just couldn't get my battered (literally) head around all this shit. It was like my life was stuck on some sort of repeat, rewind button.

Chapter Thirty-Nine

It took approximately three weeks for my face to regain a very normal expression. It took two days for my Dad's anger to hide itself deep within his bloke-ness. It took Mike half hour of playing nurse before he got bored but it took a mere hour after my beating (apparently) for Kaleigh Adams, A.K.A; love of my life to get tied up with Meeky, A.K.A; prick of a bully. Of course I didn't find out until I reluctantly went back to school when my face wasn't so severe.

Going back to school was horrible. Not as horrible as being chaperoned by Dad or Mike or Mam or even either Nan's mind. I mean, seriously, your Nan waiting outside the pans in Tescos is the right way to getting another bloody kicking. Anyway, back to school. I'd continued to keep my gob completely shut, there was no way on God's Earth was I going to let the boys get the better of me.

When I was a kid Dad and me spent one whole half term making a gambo. It was the best bloody gambo in the valley, one day I was ploughing down the foot path by my old primary school when I'd driven it over a plank of strategically placed wood. It was right in the middle of the path, right in the bloody way. I'd gone arse over head as I flew over the handle bars. Luckily, I was just grazed but the gambo had shattered into awkward pieces. As I assessed the damage, Meeky had run out from the bushes laughing his head off. The prick had done it on purpose. I'd gone home crying and Dad had offered me a little advice; 'Son, bury the hatchet and mark the spot.' At fifteen I was still marking the bloody spot. So, I would bide my time patiently and carefully until the time was right and I could trip the knob up, for ruining my gambo and my face.

Of course, this was the plan before I saw him and Kaleigh snogging in the corridor. And, let me tell you, I could have taken a thousand beatings because the pain was a walk in the rugby field compared to the punch my poor broken heart took when I caught sight of them canoodling.

I wasn't sure why it hurt so bad; was I embarrassed, you know like a loser? Had I been head over heels in love with Kaleigh or was this just what it felt like to be betrayed?

I must have just been stood there, staring. God, I hope I wasn't there long, like a bloody mouth-opened spaz or something. And it hadn't been until two massive hands had manoeuvred me into an empty classroom did I realise I'd even been moved. "J, are you OK?" my throat tightened and my chest seemed to shrink allowing my heart to pound angrily. I could feel it pumping fury into my mouth, which is not a good feeling, I can tell you.

'Top of the world.' I replied. It was Wedgy. He had the cheek to look sympathetic.

'Listen, J.'

147

'Save it. Just save it.' I started to back up.

'Look, I had nothing to do with it. I told him, I mean them, I told them to leave you alone. Next thing I know there's an ambulance on the yard.'

'Oh, so you wasn't kicking my face in then? Thanks for that.' I was practically screaming my voice was so high.

'No. I was eating a bloody prawn baguette in the canteen. I was going to come and see you, after. I seen your Dad but I wasn't sure whether you'd want to see anyone. He said, best to leave you alone anyway.' nice one Dad.

'I wasn't really in a fit state to see anyone to be honest." I'd lowered my voice but my tone was still unfriendly. I wasn't sure what to believe anymore. Who was really my friend, who wanted to stab me in the back or more seriously my heart? Who was into what, who was mad, who was sane and who had teamed up with who? It was if the world was freezing up slowly as winter swallowed up autumn and I had no control over what the fuck was happening with my life. Suddenly my face throbbed and I felt sick. The heating in the classroom was powerful and I felt myself sway.

'Are you alright, J?' Wedgy's voice was far, far away. It was somewhere in the summer, where outside was warm and classrooms were cool, with lots of air in them. "Jon?" his voice was miles away now and his body was shrinking. He had got to almost pin size when the noise, the air, the heat all disappeared.

I woke up in the office with a wet face and a sloppy, damp towel on my forehead.

'Welcome back.' it was the school nurse, it took a while for me to function and when I did I was in for a bloody shock. The school nurse was not only young she was beautiful. I'm talking movie star beautiful.

'God, J you had me scared, mate.' it was Wedgy and anybody would have sworn he had been the one to… well, whatever it was that had happened that needed medical attention. "You passed out." He was pink as pink could be with tiny beads of sweat all over his face.

'Did you hit me?' I couldn't resist the dig.

'No! no, of course I didn't you prick.' he was looking at Sienna Miller two.

'No honey, no one hit you, you just passed out. Do you mind if I ask you some questions?' she was seriously heavenly and she was touching me, fussing and touching.

'No, ask away.' I'd started squirming a bit. I mean, I really didn't want to meet my future wife in this state.

'Calm down, babe, take it easy.' she was about twenty which equals a five year age gap, which is hardly anything is it? She had perfect skin and her eyes were a perfect, sparkly blue. She was way more than Kaleigh, she was a woman not a stupid kid of a girl.

'When did you last eat, babe?' how didn't I pick up on that! She was Australian! Wow, I felt my old boy begin to perk up. "Jon, hello, what did you last eat?"

'Um...' when did I last eat? The thought of food wasn't exactly appealing. '...I'm not sure.'

'Thought so, doll. You fancy a snack?' a different kind of snack whizzed around my filthy little mind.

'Not really.' I giggled like a schoolgirl.

'Come on. I got a cheeky Mars bar in me bag.' oh my God! She was flirting with me, she wanted to give me chocolate from her bag, I couldn't help but wonder what else she wanted to give me.

'I'll have it if you don't want it, J?' Wedgy said. She looked at me, I looked at her and I swear we exchanged a knowing, it said; he really doesn't need chocolate. We had a connection, a real adult connection. It was like the stuff Mam read on holidays; *The nurse looked at her young patient, they shared a look, she felt her loins warm.'* I wasn't really sure what or where her loins were, but I'm pretty sure it was a good thing if they were warm.

'Come on Jon, eat it for me.' she pushed her bottom lip out and I got hard.

'OK.' I coughed. I was half way between eating the Mars bar and wondering Sienna's real name when there was a knock on the door.

'Come in.' even her voice was perfect, like birds singing in the morning.

It was Dad.

'Alright?' he said to me. 'Hi, I'm his Dad.' he said to my new girlfriend, and she blushed.

'Hi.' she purred in her Aussie drawl. 'I'm Sara, I'm the schools nurse.' they shook hands and she giggled. Oh no, she giggled.

'What happened, then?' Dad put his concerned parent look on. 'He need to go to hospital?'

'God no.' she flicked her hair and her eyelashes at the same time. 'Our buddy here has been skipping meals, haven't you sport?' a minute ago I was babe.

'J?' Dad was oblivious to my nurse pushing her boobs further out into her uniform.

'I, been busy.' I grinned at him.

'Now sport, you can't go skipping meals, you need to eat. Doesn't he Dad?' oh please, how obvious could she have been?

'Yes Jon, you gotta start looking after yourself.' I hadn't noticed Wedgy's disappearance out of the office.

'I didn't do it on purpose, I just sort of forgot to eat.' this all seemed slightly old school, I felt like a third bloody wheel. Sara the slapper was blatantly flirting with my Dad, did she have no shame? Giggling and flicking and posing, she even ruffled my hair at one point, cheeky bitch. I wondered whether Dad realised she was trying to get into his pants.

'He's getting married.' I hadn't meant to blurt it out, it just happened. Damn this stupid bloody verbal shits. It got worse you see, I had to add; 'To a man!'

'J.' Dad said, and I think he said it to show authority although he was grinning pretty broadly. Sara on the other hand had a look on her face that was just priceless. She sort of looked horrified, curious and a little peaky at the same time. I rammed the last bit of chocolate into my gob so I suppressed the vast amount of laughter that was trapped not only in my throat but behind my eyes and in the nooks of my brains.

'Oh.' she finally said. 'That's really nice, when's the, um, big day?' suddenly she was very busy in her box of tricks.

'In a couple of weeks.' Dad said.

'Cool. Now Jon, promise me you'll eat your brekkie, babe?' Bingo! I was babe again! 'We don't want you passing out again, do we?' God, I can't believe a minute ago I'd fancied this bird.

Chapter Forty

With my leave pass firmly in hand me and Dad laughed all the way to Nan's.

'Did you see her face?' Dad was wiping tears from hiss cheeks. 'I thought she was going to die.'

'I know." I said. 'Oh gosh, how lovely.' I'd somehow managed to master her accent. Dad slapped the steering wheel of the Bemma and howled. And then I had to ruin them moment and ask a really bloody stupid question; 'Did you fancy her though?' Dad took a double look at me.

'Are you serious?'

'I'm just curious. Before Mike she would have been right up your street.' I felt the awkwardness creep through the snazzy interior. Dad sighed.

'J. I'm gay. One hundred percent homosexual, and if I'm honest I always was.'

'Honest?'

'Yeah. I mean, don't get me wrong I loved your mother with every inch of my heart, but there was always something missing.'

'So, you always knew?'

'Yeah. I wasn't always sure what it was exactly, but I think that may have been because I sort of repressed it. You see, it's easier for some blokes to deal with.'

'Oh.' was all I could manage. So my old man had always been a bender. And, you know what; it didn't bother me in the slightest. 'I bet you're glad you met Mike then?' Dad was beaming.

'I'm very glad, J.'

Dad had said that Mike was at Nan's getting things sorted for the wedding so we had to go there. Now, not that I analyse every word uttered to me but I had expected Nan and Mike to be sorting invitations or table plans or anything that remotely involved the planning of a civil partnership. What I hadn't expected was to find Mike and Nan in some sort of show girl costumes dancing round the living room to Barry Manilows greatest hits.

'What the ...?' Dad's expression was one of pure amusement. I mean, he'd had one hell of a day, first he'd practically been propositioned by my school nurse and now he'd come home to find his recently widowed mother dancing as if in a chorus line with his fiancée, who was also dolled up as a woman in feathers and sequins. God, it really wasn't worth thinking about.

'What the hell are you pair up to?'

'Well, it's the Copa Cabana, isn't it?' Nan explained this to us as if we were supposed to know that the flamboyant costumes and blaring hi-fi were as obvious as the grass being green.

'Wanna' join in?' Mike was pretty breathless.

'What you think, J?' Dad gave me a playful nudge.

'Not on your Nelly.' I giggled. I mean, this was just nuts, bloody nuts.

'Oh, come on you bloody party poopers.' fair play they hadn't stopped on account of our arrival. Just danced, in the middle of crazy Nan's paisley, over cluttered living room.

'We haven't even had a drink yet, have we Mike?'

'Not a drop, babe. Come on boys?' still bouncing Mike turned the music up and don't ask me how or why we all ended up dancing. Right there in the living room, for ages. And do you know what; it felt bloody good.

After our dancing session (You'd never think I'd been sent home from school for collapsing would you?) Nan made us sausage, egg and chips a meal she had mastered in the chip pan. A meal that was so wrong it was right. I wolfed mine down and then I polished Mike's off.

'I couldn't possibly eat it, I've got to watch my weight, don't you know?'

We were knee deep in table plans before it struck me that I'd spent a whole day, almost whole night (it was dark outside at this point) without thinking about Kaleigh and Meeky. Obviously, Kaleigh had crossed my mind a couple of times but not in a 'Kaleigh and Meeky' together kind of way.

'Kaleigh's got a new boyfriend.' I hadn't realised I'd said it out loud.

'Oh no.' Mike looked close to tears.

'J, how come you never said?'

'I only just thought about it.'

'Oh lovey, I liked her as well, never mind strapping boy like you will find someone new in no time, you're like your Dad.' Nan looked slightly perplexed. 'Although, no offence to you two…' she gestured to Mike and Dad who were now holding hands. 'I hope you don't get a new boyfriend. I'd like a great granddaughter, see?' Everyone laughed.

'Your alright Nan, I don't fancy boys.'

'Oh good. Because my friend Barbara, you know the one with the expensive perm who speaks to dead people.' she whispered dead people, like they may get offended. 'Well, she predicted that a young girl would become part of the family and she'd bring lots of little girls. So, I've pinned my hopes on you J, considering everyone else is either loopy or bloody queer.' nice one Nan, spot on, fair play. Mike and Dad suppressed giggles and I sat there bemused and gob smacked at the same time.

'Very few girls in our family, see?'

'Well, I'll see what I can do for you Nan.' this time we all laughed. For a day that started out pretty shit it certainly ended on a high. I was starting to look forward to this wedding.

Chapter Forty-One

Research has proven that just two bananas provide enough energy for a strenuous ninety minute workout. If this was the case, little did I know, I'd need to eat at least five million bananas to get me through the next couple of days.

Chapter Forty-Two

I went to school the following Monday, energised and ready to face the world; well, ready to face the whole comp. I had even prepared myself to see the valleys answer to the new Posh and Beck's; A.KA Kaleigh and Meeky. Because I, Jonathan Jones was going to be the bigger person and rise above the fuckers.

Apparently they'd spent their first week as a couple snogging in very public places and turning up with love bites all over their necks and chests, tacky or what?

Anyway, I was going about my normal business of double science and religious education, you know normal Monday morning stuff when the strangest thing happened.

'Are you Jonathan?" Jonathan Jones?' it was Billy Edwards, (his real name was Stephen – with a PH. I'm not entirely sure why everyone calls him Billy?) Billy's in the year above me, he plays second row for Gwent County and the Dragons and he's pretty popular. How the hell he even knew my name was beyond me?

'Yeah that's me.' I felt privileged and scared and curious and …God, just ask cool Jon.

'Well, I want to shake your hand mucca. I've been faking stomach upsets since September to try and get into Sara.'

'Sara?'

'Ooh I like his style, lads.' Billy's posse had gathered behind him.

'Very non-chilount.' they all laughed and I sort of smiled. I was very confused to say the least. 'So, I heard you knocked her back, my friend.' I really wasn't sure whether I was dreaming, or maybe I'd inherited Mam's crazy gene and I was hallucinating or something?

'Um…' was all I could muster.

'Come on buddy, what happened?' I was literally surrounded by a herd of big boys all eager to hear some sort of story, but seriously my mind was blank.

'The bugger doesn't kiss and tell lads,' Billy slapped my shoulder, which kind of knocked the wind out of me. 'I like you Jon, I like your style. See you about Kid.' he gave me a parting whack and so did every one of his boys. What the bloody hell was all that about?

I was stood outside the art room kind of glued to the spot considering whether my life could get any stranger. Who the hell was Sara and when did I knock her back? I mean, really I was in no position to knock anyone back, was I? Perhaps my life had fast forwarded a couple of days, weeks or months even, maybe Dad and Mike were all ready married? Maybe I'd met this Sara at the wedding?

'What was all that about?' what was up with Wedgy interrupting my bloody staring/ thinking sessions?

'I have no idea.' he looked like a big, grinning idiot.

'Oh, so he didn't mention sexy Sara, school nurse maid then?' I literally felt the penny drop in my head.

'Sara! Of course.'

'Remember now, do you? There's been a hell of a lot of rumours going round school about you and her.' I couldn't help but smile, even though I was meant to be mad at

Wedgy, this moment was too good to pass up. I Jonathan Jones was having good rumours spread about me.

'I wonder who could have started those?' Wedgy clicked his tongue and tapped his foot. God, at this rate I'd be loaded with all these coins dropping.

'What did you do that for?'

'Thought your street cred could do with a bit of updating, boyo.' oh my god! Was this his way of apologising? He must feel really bad about beating me up, again. 'Fancy skipping art and getting pissed? My parents are at work and they've been stacking the garage with booze for Christmas?' well, I was all ready failing this year, what's another day off and I quite fancied getting drunk.

'Tidy.' I said

Chapter Forty-Three

We got steaming that afternoon and I can tell you for a fact it sure beat art and R.E. Fair play to Wedgy's parents they were like alcoholic squirrels, there was surely enough booze in their garage for at least three Christmas's.

Anyway, it was really good spending some time with the Wedgemister, because it turned out he hadn't kicked my head in the changing rooms, and he too hadn't spoken to Meeky the twat since that day.

'I told them to leave you be, but you know Meeky once he's got an idea in his head. And you know it's got jack shit to do with your Dad, this is all about Kaleigh. God, he was so angry when you and her got together.'

'But why, that boy could get any girl he wanted?'

'Doesn't matter, he wanted Kaleigh. Fancy a cider this time?'

'Yeah why not?'

And before we knew it quarter past three turned up and I had to stumble home so Mam had no idea I'd skipped school. Although, she wouldn't have noticed if I turned up in a bloody sombrero and silk frills 'cause when I eventually managed to put my key in the lock and trip into the living room the strangest of scenes awaited me.

'God, I really have had too much to drink?'

'What babe?'

'Nothing Mam.' Sprawled out in every available space on the carpet was Mam, Julie, Crazy Nan, Mike and for some odd reason Davy. They were all in a state of undress with various colours and creams spread across their skin.

'Hi J.' Mike sprung up. 'Welcome to the beauty room! Ta-da!' I hadn't immediately noticed the several empty bottles of wine and shit loads of glasses everywhere. "Would you like any treatments, Sir or perhaps I can interest you in a cheeky glass of vino?" Now he was talking my language.

'What's going on then?' I finally asked.

'We're having a pre wedding pamper session, babe.' Mam's eyes were sparkly, a sure sign of intoxication, or were mine sparkly, another sure sign of intoxication "Just for the girls and Mike." Davy and his pink toenails coughed. 'Oh and Davy's helping us pick colours. He's been very helpful, haven't you babe?' I sort of did a manly nod that was completely lost on Davy as looked very pleased with himself and his toenails.

'Come and sit by me, Luvvy.' Nan looked in her element. She had both multi-coloured feet on separate foot stools and two glasses of some sort of curious looking cocktails in both multi-coloured hands. 'How was school, have you seen that bitch?' fair play to Nan she never stood on ceremony.

'No, haven't seen her yet, not bothered either Nan.'

'That's my boy, move on. Julie would you mind putting some music on, lets have a proper party, is it?' everyone mutually agreed a party was a F.A.B idea (Fucking, Awesome, Brainwave as Davy kindly informed us.) So, Julie put a party album on and before I knew it Mam, Mike, Nan, Julie and bloody Davy were doing their best

impression of the village people to none other, than
Y.M.C.A! And I wasn't sure whether it was the afternoon
alcohol intake or just the complete lunacy of the situation
but I nearly pissed myself laughing.

After they'd bopped and screamed the lyrics to about four
or five more tunes and I'd consumed a further three or four
drinks everyone breathlessly flopped and turned the music
down.

'Ooh, I'll suffer tomorrow.' Nan said whilst topping up
her sex on the beach with a bottle of chardonnay. 'Never
mind, it's only once your son gets married to another bloke,
ey?' everyone, including Mike cracked up. 'Well, I hope
this is the last time he gets hitched, I mean he's had a
woman, a man he'll marry the bloody dog next time
round.' again everyone laughed. I laughed so hard and for
so long before I knew it I was crying and everyone was
staring at me and appropriately the music had stopped so it
looked worse than it was.

'J, what's wrong babe?' Mam had manoeuvred to me
and was stroking my head. (Sign of seriousness of
situation.) 'Come on he won't really marry an animal.'
now, looking back I can say it with ease; I was crying
because I was pissed, pissed as a newt I think the saying
goes but at the time surrounded by a pile of crazy people I
was happy. It was plain and simple, things were on the up
and it had been so long since I had just been happy that it
hit me like a full on smack.

'It's nothing.' I was sobbing at this point. Proper,
breathless tears.

'Would you like me to…' hiccup, '…Sing you a song,
babes?' Julie could hardly keep her head up which made
me cry/ laugh/ breathe more. 'OK, '*The sun come out…*'
hiccup, '*tomorrow….*' hiccup, '*when I think of a day…*'
hiccup, 'Bugger, I forgot the words.' I couldn't take much
more of this I was ready to combust.

'I think that's making him worse sweetie?' Mike was on his knees too. 'Is it Kaleigh?' I managed to shake my head.

'It's just…'

'Come on, babes.'

'I'm just happy, I guess.' my crying eased up. God, you'd swear I was half gay at least.

'Oh … that's so…' and before he could finish his sentence Mike was crying like a baby.

'Oh dear.' Mam was wiping her eyes.

'This is beautiful!' Julie joined in.

'Have we got anymore wine, please?' Nan was completely un-fazed by the emotion and Davy was sticking Wotsits in every hole on his face. Then the door bell went.

'Oh shit!' Mam wiped her eyes and made for the door and Julie, Mike and myself tried as best we could to compose ourselves. I could hear a mans mumble and Mam's pitch got slightly higher.

'Who'd you reckon it is?' Mike was theatrically tissueing his face and sniffing, he really would make a good actor. 'Perhaps it's your Dad?' he looked hopeful.

Now, to say I was a bit pessimistic about the whole fate, universe controls and karma bull shit was a bit of an understatement and when you look back on the couple of months I've had you'll probably think, 'no wonder' because whenever and I mean when-ever things start to look up something comes along to fuck the feel good situation right up. Like the pamper session night. Misery turned up in the form of Doctor Atwood with two suitcases and a way too full Morrison's carrier bag.

'She's kicked me out. For good. Hello everyone.' he gave us all a pansy wave as he de-steamed his spectacles. 'She said it couldn't work and that I should just leave, so I came here.'

'Oh.' said Mam.

'Glass of wine luvvy?' said Nan.

'Poor baby.' said Mike.

159

'I've got a Wotsit stuck.' said Davy and Julie snorted in her sleep.

What a bloody fuck up. Stage enter; new father.

'I don't want to impose. But we are engaged?' Oh heck! 'So, if it's not too much trouble, would it be possible if you could, if you wouldn't mind that is, if I could stay here for a while.' it was the most I'd ever heard the bloke say.

'Oh, well...' Mam looked around the room until she caught my eye. I dutifully nodded. 'OK. I suppose it'll be nice to have a man about again.'

'And he can dose you up to keep you sane.' Nan was sipping her concoctions through a straw. Mike looked disgusted as he eyed up Doctor A's shoes. 'Actually I'm running a bit low on Valium. I only slept for thirteen hours last night, I like a good seventeen, makes me feel younger, see.' she continued slurping.

'Nan, ssshh.' God she'd be in a straight jacket if good old Graham heard that.

'I don't want to interrupt your... your party. Shall I come back?'

'Nonsense!' Mike poured the Doc some cocktails and sat him next to Julie. 'You will be coming to the wedding wont you, Doctor?'

'Yes he will.' Mam answered, smiling. 'And then you can come to ours, right Gray?' Christ not another bloody wedding.

'Indeed.' he said and then the strangest thing happened to his face, at first it looked as if it was in spasm but then I realised he was smiling, God, I really hoped he wasn't about to mess Mam about again or worse she tie him up or dress him up or whatever weird tricks she had in her box!

'Let's play twister!' Julie's mad, red head had erected itself as she declared naked twister was far more fun.

Chapter Forty-Four

I was too hung over to go school on Tuesday so, at this point my annual attendance was abysmal, or very shitty as I'd prefer to say. And to be honest, I might as well have had the Wednesday, Thursday and bloody Friday off because I was like a wank stain in all my subjects. Everything had been turned upside down. Doctor A had moved in and along with him came funny phone calls, threatening letters and even decapitated teddy bears came through the letter box. No prizes for guessing his ex wife (or even Marion, the mother in law) was a little bitter. Now, as if one new person in residence wasn't enough Mike decided to temporarily move in too gushing that it was probably super lucky to not see his future spouse for at least three days before the wedding.

'I mean, there's hardly any superstitions for civil partnerships, is there?' he continued to describe his lucky and un-lucky in-depth theories at the breakfast bar, wearing a silk purple dressing gown, a matching eye mask and the same colour fluffy slippers.

And as if all this mayhem wasn't enough I had to work on my best man speech which even the thought of getting up and speaking was making me more and more nauseous by the minute. I mean, what the fucking hell was I supposed to say? 'Well done boys, have fun and thanks for the cheese and pineapples.'

Anyway, as the wedding loomed closer and my sanity further and further away both Meeky and Kaleigh and Mam and Doctor Atwood seemed to get stronger. God, it was actually quite sickening to witness. Meeky and Kaleigh hand in hand, tongue in tongue all around school and then I'd come home to Mam and the Doctor in a tangle of limbs looking embarrassed as I cough loudly or slam doors or both if they were really involved. Yuck! And, as if that wasn't bad enough Mike spent the whole time prancing round with various smelling face masks on singing bloody Abba songs.

On the Thursday before the wedding I decided enough was enough I needed some bloke time.

'Are ewe sure J?'

'Yes Steve, all off.'

'Well, this is a turn out for the books, boy.' I heard him turn the shaver on and my stomach did a loop to loop. I hope I didn't end up looking like a hooligan, like part of the bloody Soul Crew or something.

'Definite now boy?'

'Go for it.'

"Well, its different buddy." Steve brushed my back down.

"Certainly is Steve." I ran my hand over my head. It felt good I had to admit. I felt lighter, like, and I know this sounds stupid, but it was as if a huge weight had been lifted. Which, realistically it had. God, I wished I'd had this done weeks ago.

'So, what's this all about then, JJ?'

'Just, fancied a change, Steve.' And change it was. I looked older, harder in fact. A grown up thug.

'Well, that's nice, boy. How's the wedding plans going. Its close now isn't it?'

'Saturday.'

'Bloody hell that came round fast.'

'Yeap, and I'm best man.'

'Well, there's an honour kid.'

'I know, I'm dead nervous, haven't a clue what to say."

'It'll come boy, ewe'll be surprised once ewe start speaking how easy it'll flow. I was best man once, loved it, everyone buys ewe beer.'

'What was your speech like?'

'Cant remember boy, I was pissed.'

Chapter Forty-Five

I tried everything to conjure up some inspiration for my speech. Literally. I flipped through magazines and books I went for a walk – I went right to the top of the bloody mountain behind our bloody house where the view is absolutely beautiful, but still nothing came. I scoured the net, looked at bold colours (said to be v. inspirational) read poetry, (honest) I had a cold shower which was horrible, I even put on one of Mam's soppy love albums but still nothing came to me.

Seriously, what was I supposed to say about two men (one being my father) getting hitched? I wasted at least three or four trees, for definite, writing and re-writing and I only seemed to get to 'ladies and gentlemen' and 'thanks for coming. Cheers.'

And have you ever 'Goggled' GAY, MAN, WEDDING. God, I'm sure Mam should have some sort of parental lock on the type of websites that came up.

And the closer the wedding got (I was counting hours and minutes at this point) the more stressed I was getting and the bigger my bloody writers block got.

The Friday night before the wedding every household that was merely connected with the wedding party was chaotic. There were ribbons and suit bags and champagne in every available crack of Mam's, Nan's, Dad's and even Julie's next door. Everyone seemed to be on very sharp pins. What's the saying; 'tempers were frayed.' Is it?

I'd all ready been involved in three arguments. The first with Mike. Apparently I was hanging about in the kitchen for far too long.

'Bloody hell Jonathan.' he'd said. 'Exactly how long does it take to scramble a bloody egg.' with that he'd huffed off to give himself a MAN-icure. (He emphasised the 'man' bit claiming his gay ancestors had invented the finger/ hand make over for blokes and women had blatantly stolen the process.)

The second argument was purely my fault. I was reading up on great inspiring speeches when Mam floated past humming/ singing some pansy love song. At first I let it go but you know what its like when you can hear something and you try and ignore it, before you know it, it's the loudest most annoying noise I ever heard. Mam had every right to call me an irrational little shit.

The third row was more amusing than serious, Nan as in Crazy Nan, asked me to sneak her a cheeky Pina Colada, which under normal circumstances would not have been a problem but Dad had enforced a strictly no-alcohol-what-so-ever law upon her.

'But please J, just a sneaky one.'

'I can't Nan.'

'The bloody cheek of it all, I nursed you, changed your nappies and listened to you whine about that little tart Kaleigh and you can't even ...help me with my knitting.'

'I didn't know you were knitting babe.'

'Yes Mike.' answered an incredibly sheepish Nan. 'I'm making you two love birds a throw for over your bed.' she gave him her best false teeth grin.

'A woollen one?' Mike looked disgusted.

'Yes...with love hearts on it.' Nan bounced off unsuccessfully; dry and angry I might add.

Now, if emotions were running this high the day before the big bash, I could only imagine what in hells teeth was in store for the actual day itself.

I decided to cut my losses and head to Dad's earlier than planned. I thought; I know, I'll work on my speech, have a beer, me and the old man could watch a dead blokey film then hit the hay all ready and refreshed for the big day. It turned out Dad had other ideas.

'You're early.' he said as I bundled my suit, my entire DVD collection, a pillow (Mike and Dad had horrible trendy thin things that were hardly worthy of being labelled a sheet let alone a pillow) and my training bag filled with spare clothes for whatever lay ahead. I even had my swimming trunks, 'cause you never know! 'And equipped for a hike by the seems.'

'Our house is mental. I still haven't finished my speech and I'm starving.'

'OK, buddy. Come in.' he made me some sort of weird curry, that 'Mike swears by for nerves' and he'd bought some low alcohol beer in for me especially. 'We can't have you smashed the night before my wedding, can we buddy?' and there was me thinking we could get messed right up and turn up at the ceremony pissed. Can you imagine?

'So, you're having trouble with your speech, then?' Dad was washing up the dishes, and I couldn't help being a tad (only a tad, mind) bitter, he never, ever did the domesticated thing when he lived with us.

'It's really hard!'

'Well, just say what you feel.'

'Hi, ladies and gentlemen I'm shit scared and slightly embarrassed t be stood up here speaking, hope you like the free wine!' There is free wine, right?'

'Yeah, there's free wine, kid.'

'Oh good.'

'It doesn't have to be gushy or over the top, just say thanks and you hope we have a long, lovely life together, slip a joke in and thank the bridesmaids.'

'You've got bridesmaids?'

'they're not real bridesmaids, they're not kitted out in dresses or anything.'

'Oh heck.'

'J, it'll be fine, honest.' alright for him to say that, he was already making a tit out of himself by marrying a bloody fella. I still had an ounce of street cred I wouldn't mind holding on to. Suddenly, I felt my chest tighten and my face burn. Shit, I really hadn't considered this whole best man thing, I mean, it was one thing standing at the alter or whatever they bloody stood at, handing rings over, it was a completely different thing to stand in a room full of people telling them how wonderful it was my Dad's decided to shag a man for the rest of his life. There is no way I could do it.

'J, don't look so worried. Now how'd you fancy some ice cream and a Rocky film?'

'Tidy.'

Oh shit!!

Chapter Forty-Six

I didn't sleep at all that night. Well, I say I didn't sleep I must have dropped off because I had horrible, horrible, nightmares about my head coming off during my best man speech, then I dreamt there were loads of catholic priest things campaigning about gay's; they were telling me that I may as well shag blokes too, then they threw red paint over me for some reason. I must have had anti-fur campaigners on my mind too.

I kept staring at the digital clock and counting how many minutes of sleep I could sneak in, but my eyes were wide open and so was my brain. Whoever said counting helps you get to sleep - lied. Because once I started counting I just wanted to carry on counting until I got to some sort of impossible bloody number.

At three forty five exactly and a couple of seconds I decided to get up and pee. I didn't really need to go I was just hoping the walk to the pan would get me so knackered I'd fall back into bed into a lovely, nice dreamy sleep. The floor downstairs was really cold on my bare feet which got me really worked up; I was even more awake after I'd hopped to the bathroom. And it was as I was peeing (turned out I did need to go a little bit) I had a stupid idea to switch my mobile on. I was sure it was at the bottom of my training bag.

Now, honest to god I wasn't expecting any messages or anything I just thought, well I don't know why I wanted to turn the bloody thing on, but it went from a simple idea to a serious urge to find it and switch it on. God, I couldn't even tell you the last time I'd even looked at it.

And then it happened.

BEEP. BEEP.

One Message Received.

'J, you should be sleeping!' shit.

'Sorry Dad.'

BEEP.BEEP.

Two Messages Received.

'Jon!' shit. Bugger.

'Sorry.'

'Turn it off and get some bloody sleep.' I put the phone under my pillow and turned it on silent. And good job I did 'cause loads of messages and missed call alerts came through. Bloody hell when did I last turn the thing on? Dad's very white spare bedroom glowed blue with my v. busy phone. Wow, who the hell had been trying to get hold of me? Then my stomach did that mankey lurch thing it does if you're on a big ride, or jumping off a cliff, or very tall building. What shit would these messages bring now? I assessed the situation as it was. I could just switch the phone back off and try my hardest to get some shut eye? No, no the seed had definitely been planted I had to read the texts. Whatever it was I'd deal with it. Oh god, I felt sick. Sick as a pig.

I'm sorry. He's a knob can't believe he beat you up. I'm so sorry xxx

J, I've finished with him. He told me everything. I'm really sorry TMB xxxx

Look I know you h8 me but I'm sorry. K xx

You have a missed call from: Kaleigh mob.

You have a missed call from: Unknown.

You have a missed call from: Meeky Home.

Why won't you answer? X

Have a good wedding. I'm sorry K xx

You have a missed call from: Unknown.

She's all yours.

Oh my god. Oh shit. What the fuck? I re-read the messages. Then I re-read them again and by the time I'd pretty much pieced everything together it was getting light outside. Oh my god. I didn't have a tired bone in my body. What was I supposed to do should I text her back? Ring her? Oh my god! And what did Meeky want, a fucking medal for good friend award? 'She's yours' My arse. Oh my god! And then another one came through.

HI! How come you're turning your phone on in the middle of the night? X

Oh Jesus Christ! She's texting me now, now this minute. She must have those delivery report things. What the fuck do I say?

Can't sleep. Wedding 2mrw. How r u?

How are you? Could I get any lamer? You dumped me, went out with my friend, or ex friend who beat fuck into me and I'm casually asking how you are in the middle of the bloody night or morning, whatever you class quarter to six as. I'm glad I didn't put a kiss in at least that way I preserved a bit of manliness.

One message received.

I've missed you xxx

Cheeky bitch. Oh god but I've missed her. What a fuck up. Part of me wanted to bounce on the bed and punch the air and the other part wanted to crawl under the squared patterned duvet and never get up. What was I supposed to say? Did she want me to say I'd missed her to and that I forgive her and would she come round to my Dad's and give me a blow job? (that last bit was a joke) or should I call her a bitch tell her she'd broken my heart and I never wanted to see her again, apart from when she comes round to give me a blow job? (Again, a joke) I decided on a bit of the truth.

I've missed u 2 but u proper messed with my head.
Simple and true and not too gay.
One Message Received.
Oh heck she was quick.
I'm really sorry. Can I see you? Xx
When? Now? Maybe a blow job wasn't out of the question.
One Message Received.
Where r u? x
And the next bit was a bit of a blur. I put my joggers and trainers on. Then I was in the park by Dad's. And then Kaleigh turned up. It was really cold and there was dew and mist all at the same time on the grass in the park. The birds had started their croaking and the only noise was Dai the milk on his arthritic old float. She looked beautiful. She had a white hoodie on, pink tartan PJ bottoms and those Ugg boot slipper things. She wasn't wearing a scrap of make up, she looked heaven sent, which really did make me think I was dreaming.

It was awkward at first. I mean, we had no where to sit because everything was damp and cold and we agreed neither of us wanted to risk piles.

'Your hair's nice.' She was blushing. 'Really suits you. You look loads older.'

'Yeah, fancied a change.' We nodded at each other for the best part of a minute after that. God, if only she was minging and stupid, I could tell her to piss off and leave me alone. But seriously, she looked so beautiful that morning.

'Look J...'

'Kaleigh...' Typical! 'Go on.'

'I'm really sorry. I had no idea he beat you up. And I'm sorry about overreacting about the wedding invite it was stupid.'

'I'm sorry I lied about... well, you know.'

'And I'm sorry I ever went out with Meeky. It was only to get back at you.' I smiled, I couldn't help it, what she was saying was like music to my ears. She was seeing him to spite me!

'It worked.' then she smiled.

'Look...' what? What did I want to say? I love you! Bit heavy. I really like you! Bit primary school. 'Kaleigh... look.' and then she kissed me! Her hands were around my neck and she was kissing me, in her pyjamas in the park in the early hours of the morning and it felt amazing. Truly amazing!

'I've still got that dress if you still need a guest for today.' and then I kissed her.

Chapter Forty-Seven

It was the photographers that eventually woke me up, yes they'd hired professional photographers. (The professionals consisted of two very camp fellas that were on Mike's photography course. This was their first real gig they told me and they were like kids in a sweet shop.)

Typical wasn't it; I got in just after seven from the park, the park that changed my life, I jumped back into Dad's spare bed which looked completely different now, and I was knocked out, dead to the world until Marty one (yes, the other one was a Marty two) woke me with his poxy flash.

'Eeerrrggghhh. What's the time?' oh to only have another cheeky hour, or even half, I'm not greedy.

'Its ten past eight, mate. Come on give us a cheeky smile for the camera.' click, Flash, Click.

'Piss off!' I really wasn't in the mood for a gay wedding.

'Jon, watch your language.'

'Sorry.' at least I'd had a solid hour in the last twenty four, I suppose that was something at least.

'*I'm getting married in the morning...ding dong the bells are gonna' chime...* Come on best man lets get you shit, showered and shaved.' oh fuck. Best man. Best man speech. Oh fuck.

'Dad...'

'Yes, son?' God, he was chirpy, far too chirpy for this time of the morning.

'Dad, about the wedding,'

'The wedding? As in today wedding?' he looked momentarily panicked.

'Yes...um...Kaleigh's coming.' how was I supposed to tell him that A. I didn't want to be bloody best man and B. I didn't have a bloody best man speech.

'Oh, so that was the bloody beeping in the middle of the night. You're a dark horse, JJ. That's my boy.' holy shit I was screwed.

Now, I'm not vain and by no means am I full of myself but I'd just like to say; the day my father got married I did him proud. I looked bloody good I gotta be honest. We'd all had matching suits tailor made by some hot designer from the city and they were sharp as...well, they were very sharp indeed. And with my new hair cut I looked like a proper man, a bloke even. The boy had finally grown up.

Dad's house was buzzing. Between the photographers taking shots of every poxy second, Clive, Steve the Barber all trying to work out where to put their flowers and a couple of non-judgemental rugby boys who'd agreed to be ushers , and who'd all ready got through three crates of cider. It was non-stop action.

When I finally emerged from the bedroom in my million dollar suit, Dad looked like he was about to cry. Clive shook my hand and one of the rugby lads handed me a can.

'You look amazing, Jon.' he eventually said. He was biting his lip and not looking at my face. 'This means so much to me, kid.' and with that he patted my back and hurried off to do something that looked important but probably wasn't.

When everyone was finally suited and booted with their carnations in the correct holes, we all posed on the decking in Dad's back yard for manly photos. And the mood was merry, and I almost managed to push the niggling, sick feeling I was experiencing due to the massive lack of speech situation, to the back of my very sleepy head.

The cars were due to pick us up at half eleven and to pass the time all us boys sat in the front room and did what men do best. We watched VH1's one hundred greatest love songs and consumed several bottles of champagne. Dad, kept rubbing his hands together and the rugby lads insisted on singing, loudly to whichever power ballad graced Dad's plasma. And then the phone rang.

'Hello...yeah, yeah....I see, is she OK? Right, so everything's under control? OK, thanks. OK, see you there.' he put the receiver down and I knew whatever was coming was not good. You know when you can tell something's wrong, I swear the atmosphere in the room just evaporated. Dad rubbed his eyes. 'J, it's your Mam.' Oh Christ. Just as you get one parent under control the other fucker goes crazy. I wonder what she'd done this time. I expect Doctor Atwood was wearing fake whiskers and was chained up a tree somewhere. "She's gone missing, J. Nobody's seen her since last night.' great, crazy Mam's gone walkabout and of all bloody days to go for a fucking wander on Dad's poxy 'gay' wedding day.

'Jeez...'

'It'll be Ok. Julie and your Auntie Lisa have gone to look for her, and everyone's on stand by. She'll be fine.' just bloody tremendous! As if this wedding needed another element of bastard craziness, Mam has gone an added a little bit more to the bill.

'I'd better go look.'

'J, the cars will be here any minute.'

'I'll meet you there. I promise.'

'Jonathan?'

'Dad, I have to find her.' and with that I left. I left in my full wedding attire to look for my crazy Mam who could be absolutely any bloody where.

Chapter Forty-Eight

I know it was the least of my worries, but I was super concerned about sweating in my suit. I mean, I wanted to look hot to trot when I turned up at the rugby club (That's where the service and reception was being held, by the way) as grown up, non-gay, best man. And if I'm totally honest I really wanted to look gorgeous and sophisticated, a bit like a mini James Bond for a certain Miss Adams.

Unfortunately my teenage body had other ideas and even though there was still frost on windscreens and it was bloody cold, power walking up and down the terraced streets of my valley was making me perspire. I wonder if I'd have a leg or armpit to stand on if I sued the deodorant company?

Where the hell was she? I looked like a compete tit shouting 'Mam' dressed like a poxy penguin. This was way beyond the call of both son, and best man duty, I swore when I found her I was gonna let rip, I would tell her how incredibly selfish she was bi-polar or no bloody bi-polar I couldn't give a flying fuck.

'JJ.' bollocks I'd been so concerned with finding my Mam, I hadn't even realised whose street I was in. 'Shouldn't you be at the wedding?'

'My Mam's gone missing.' Meeky was in joggers, he had no top on and even though my suit probably cost more than his mothers terrace I felt suddenly felt shabby and a bit chubby. God, how was he so cut?

'Oh. Sorry, mate. You need a hand looking for her?'

'Not off you. No.' God, did those words just come out of my mouth? And I didn't want to stop there. 'Or, do you want to help so you can beat the shit out of me round the corner?'

'J, look…'

'Or maybe you'd like to steal my Mam and claim her as yours if we find her?'

'I'm sorry J, I…'

'Save it, I haven't got the time.' I started to walk fast up his street, I heard his gate open and click shut and then;

'J…' bang. I hadn't meant to but I smashed him straight in his face, and apart from my fist throbbing it felt pretty good. "FUCK!" he was clutching his face and sort of spinning on the pavement. 'Fuck, fuck, FUCK!'

'Whoops I slipped.' and with that I walked away, with a little grin on my face. God, I hoped he bruised.

I found Mam in the Post Office. I know, off all bloody places? I'd actually gone in for a bottle of water and there she was talking as happy as Larry with Shilpa. She was decked out in her 'sort of, but not' bridesmaid dress thing and was just happily gossiping about the community centres bingo night. She was normal Mam.

'Mam!'

'JJ, hey babe. What are you doing here?'

'Me? What the hell are you doing here? Everyone's looking for you.'

'Oh dear.' Shilpa chipped in.

'Why? I had to post my prescription off, or I'll have no medication, and we don't want that do we?' She giggled. 'I need my medication you see.' Shilpa nodded as if she too needed a high dosage of Valium and Lithium or whatever

174

else Mam dosed up on. 'I also went to the hairdressers, you like?' She asked either of us. 'I feel it's important to have your hair done for occasions like this I mean…'

'What time is it, please Shilpa?'

'It is eleven forty five.'

'Shit Mam, we've got to go.'

'Watch your language J.'

'Sorry.' it took me a further ten minutes to get Mam out of the bloody Post Office, god the medication made her way too laid back for her own good.

The service was due to start at half twelve and the rugby club was at least a half hour walk, so it was do-able but tight.

'Come on Mam.' she clicked in her heels about ten paces behind me.

'Jonathan, you seem really worked up?' she'd stopped in her tracks. Jesus this was no time for a heart to heart. 'Is everything, alright?'' Alright? Alright? Was this woman's serious for Christ sake? We had hardly any time at all to make it to her ex-husbands gay wedding, where I was best bloody man and her 'sort of' bloody bridesmaid and she wanted a deep and meaningful chin wag in the middle of town.

'I'm fine Mam, honest. But, we gotta get to the club.'

'Is this about Kaleigh?!' shit I was meant to meet Kaleigh in the car park.

'No, Mam, Kaleigh's coming t the wedding now.'

'Oooh good!' she clapped her hands. 'That's lovely, oh god I could cry.'

'Can you cry and walk please Mam, we're gonna be really late and I'm best Man.'

'Yes, yes sorry I'm just so excited.' progress she'd started moving. One step, two step, that's the girl, three step. 'I can't wait for my wedding, with Graham, he's lovely isn't he? You do like him, don't you J?' AAAaaaarrrrhhhhhh!

'He's great Mam. The nicest bloke I've ever met. Now please, if you don't hurry, I'm gonna go on with out you.' her bottom lip started to quiver.

'You don't like him do you?'

'MAM! He's marvellous, but now's not the time.' she was fully blown crying now. God, why me? Seriously Why me? 'I'm sorry, Mam. I think you and him will have an amazing life together, you're perfect for each other, just like Dad and Mike. Now, let's go let them have their special day.'

'Oh that's lovely J; I'm really looking forward to your speech, later.' shit the speech. Shit the speech. Shit the bollocking speech.

Chapter Forty-Nine

When we finally got to the Rugby Club, Kaleigh wasn't in the car park. There were, however, several clusters of very eccentric looking groups of people, chatting loudly and smoking cigarettes, I recognised a couple of them from Dad and Mikes stag party. Mam breathlessly clip clopped behind me waving like the Queen of bloody Sheba, to anyone who gave her half a glance. "She'd also acquired an upper class, lady of leisure accent as she; 'Hi' ('ed) people.

'Where the hell have you been?' Dad hissed through his new, very expensive super white smile. 'Is she having a turn?'

'No, she was in the Post Office.'

'The Post Office? What the... Hi, Fiona, Where's Cosmo?' A lady in a pink rubber dress and one of those umbrella hat things explained the whereabouts of Cosmo in a really funny accent, which gave me the perfect opportunity to sneak off and try to find Kaleigh.

Seriously, if I hadn't been there I wouldn't have believed this wedding. There were people there that looked like they should have been on day release from the asylum, not wedding guests and the worse thing about it was, half these people were of 'incredible cultural importance' so Mike rammed down my throat at every possible name dropping opportunity.

I'd made my way inside the function room, where a fake alter thing had been set up for the nuptials. And, I had to admit the club had come up trumps. The place looked spectacular, I say that in a manly voice whilst scratching my balls, mind. There were dark red flowers and some sort of ivy thing, I think, wrapped round seats, and table legs and every available wrapping device, all over the ceiling were twinkling fairy lights. Fair play, the place looked good.

'Hi, sexy.' now, if I could keep any memory, saved in a perfect little carved box in a special room in my brain, it would be the morning I turned round before my fathers gay wedding and knew one hundred percent I was in love, pure and simple, perfect young love.

She was the most beautiful thing I had ever laid eyes on.

'Oooh, you are looking hot, babe.' I looked hot, I looked hot, Kaleigh was there and she thought I looked hot.

'You scrubbed up pretty good yourself, Miss Adams.' she did a twirl and oh my god did she look good. She was wearing a shiny, pearly dress and her hair was all curly and hanging over her beautiful shoulders. I made my way towards her, and for a freaky, other universe, crazy 'what if' moment it was like I was walking up the aisle towards the girl of my dream. God I loved her.

'I love you too.' heck, had I said it out loud? I really should ask Doctor A about this not sure whether I said or not issue. 'I'm so glad we're back together.'

'Me too.' and then we kissed, in the middle of a fake church, with twinkling lights and flowers. It was perfect. Absolutely perfect until;

'J, quick, your needed out there, Mike's arrived. Hi, Kaleigh love, you look lovely, come sit by me I've got my hip flask and some humbugs.' nice one Nan.

The function room looked like an over priced rainbow once filled and Dad's face also went through a couple of rainbow shades as we waited in the front row for his future bride/ groom, whatever Mike wanted to be labelled.

'Shit, shit, shit.' Dad mumbled.

'It's OK, Dad, calm down.' I whispered.

'Christ, why am I so nervous?'

'Um, 'cause your getting married?'

'Shit.' I rubbed his shoulder because that's what the best man does in films.

'Its OK mun, you'll be fine.' Dad's eyes welled up a bit and he bit his lip, I patted his back. 'Man up.'

'Excuse me?'

'I said man up for Christ sake.'

'Man up?'

'Yes, for god sake.' and with that I saw Dad's shoulders relax, his eyes dried up and he started beaming at me. Shit I was good, I wonder if there was a profession in this type of work?

'Thanks Jon. You mean the world to me.' and with that Brian Adams started screaming out of the PA system as Mike also in a v. expensive suit, made his way to the front of the make-shift church. And then the music stopped and so the rest of my Dad and Mike's life began.

'We are gathered here to unite the two of you in marriage, which is an institution ordained by the state and made honourable by the faithful keeping of good men and women throughout all ages, and is not to be entered into lightly or unadvisedly.' I couldn't have summed it up better myself. I mean, at first, and well, to be honest up until the strange looking vicar/ Disc jockey just hit the nail on the head, I was not so sure about this civil ceremony shit but who said a girl had to fall in love with a boy or a boy fall in love with a girl? And if you looked at Dad and Mike, in all honesty they were pretty perfect for each other even thought they went dead against the grain.

I turned round to give Kaleigh a wink and my tummy flipped. Everything had come full circle, Mam and Doctor Atwood, or Graham as I would have to start calling him pretty soon were mooching up at each other and my girl was all smiles and curls and everyone who mattered to me was looking, well, half amused and half happy but happy never the less.

And then it hit me, life is what you make of it and who gave jack shit about what anyone else thought because deep down they weren't even interested. What mattered was Numero uno and his or hers nearest and dearest.

'Neil, do you take Mike to be your wedded husband? To have and to hold, to love and to cherish, in sickness and in health, in times of good and bad?'

'I, Neil, pledge to you, Mike, as my friend, my love, and my companion to love, honour, and cherish as long as we both shall live.'

'I, Mike, pledge to you, Neil, as my friend, my love, and my companion to love, honour, and cherish as long as we both shall live.' they said the next bit in perfect harmony as they slipped god only knows how many thousand pounds worth of rings on their fingers;

'I give this ring in token and in pledge of my constant faith and abiding love with all that I am, and all that I will become.'

'OK, then Kids, I now pronounce you cool, hip fellas man and man. Rock on! You may kiss the groom.'

Everyone whooped and applauded as Dad and Mike exited the function room to one of the Beach Boy's classics. Then we all had to stand out front and have photos taken and I swear half the valley were in the car park to witness this very strange wedding. Even the local paper had turned up and a very prestigious magazine was doing a piece on gay weddings. God, I felt like a P list (at least) celebrity.

'Ladies and Gentlemen, if you'd like to make your way into the reception hall where we will toast the bride and groom to their future together, and then dinner will be served.'

Chapter Fifty

High in fibre; including bananas in the diet can help restore normal bowel action helping to overcome the problem without restoring to laxatives.

I'd been fine throughout the ceremony, I'd been fine getting people to their tables, I'd been fine kissing Kaleigh in front of everyone and then my stomach did that gurgle thing. Had I, in my state of weird non-sleep the night before consume a pile of bananas so that conveniently, or non-conveniently, (however you look at it) I had a bout of the runs just before the toast.

There was no way I could say what I felt with crap running down my designer trouser leg, was there?

Final Whistle

DING DING

Ladies and Gentlemen: can I have your attention please? Thanks. OK, so most of you know me already but for those of you who don't; I'm Jonathan, Neil's son and well, Mikes step son now, I think. (APPALUSE)

OK, before I forget, I'll do the thank yous. Firstly; thanks for everyone who turned up and has made this day extra special for both my father and Mike. Thanks to the beautiful 'sort-of' bridesmaids Julie and my Mam. You look lovely ladies. (APPLAUSE) A thank you to all who have made this service possible, the caterers, the bar-staff, keep it coming guys. (APPLAUSE AND LAUGHTER) I'd also like to thank both my Nan's and Clive for providing extra houses for the vast amount of preparation this wedding needed. Also, thanks to D.J Monkey, who conducted the ceremony, you did a great job buddy. Finally, and most of all, a big thanks to Mike for making my father one incredibly happy fella. Well done. (APPLAUSE)

Now generally when someone is asked to be best man they're over the moon; Firstly because your friend slash Dad is marrying the 'bloke' of his dreams (LAUGHTER) and secondly that he's asked *me* to be best man. He's actually trusted me with the responsibility of not messing up his wedding day! Don't worry there's still time yet Dad. (LAUGHTER)But seriously, to put into words, to sum this whole thing up has been one of the hardest things I've ever had to do. For a start how the hell do you sum up love? Well, one Googled quote describes love as 'a journey not a destination.' And what a journey Dad and Mike's love has been so far. God help the next couple of decade's boys if the last year or so is anything to go by! (LAUGHTER) Only joking guys!

But in all honesty, It's been one hell of a ride as most of you know. For a start, I bet a couple of months ago you'd never think I'd have even attended this wedding let alone be best man, but I'm glad I'm here and I'm glad Dad and me are back on track, after all you only get one chance at life and you definitely only get one Dad, although In time I'll be happy to class mike, as an extra Dad, if he'll have me that is? (APPLAUSE)

Right, where do I start? Well, as best man I'm supposed to not be too 'gushy', say what I feel and I'm meant to tell you very embarrassing stories about the groom. Which groom I hear you ask! (APPLAUSE) I'm also supposed to miss out anything to do with ex girlfriends, apparently that's a no-no, and also really not a problem at this wedding, is it? (LAUGHTER AND APPLAUSE)

So, lets start with before Mike and Dad got together well, before Dad met Mike he was straight, or straight-ish at least, although I'm sure you all had your doubts, Dad went to my school and I've seen what's written behind the bike sheds Mr! (LAUGHTER) But, seen's as he was married to my Mam, there are no ex boyfriends to shamefully bring up, at least I don't think there are, answers on a post card please,(LAUGHTER) and considering I wasn't about when my old man was sewing his wild oats I cant tell you about any of his drunken conquests or antics. I can however, tell you some stories from when I was younger. (OOOs and ARRRs) Don't look so worried Dad I won't mention the Wham incident. (LAUGHTER)

Some of my fondest memories of Dad as I was growing up were the legendry Saturday night rows him and my Mam had after he came back from rugby. I'm sure they are probably some of Julie's favourite memories too, how many times did you have to call the police Jul? (LAUGHTER)Julie lives next door, through the very thin walls for those of you who don't know. Remember the night you peed all over Mam, Dad? That was probably my favourite memory. (LAUGHTER) How many plates do you reckon were smashed that night? Not to mention the TV that got stumbled into and the vase Nan brought us back from Spain, dropped. Whoops, sorry Nan. (LAUGHTER) We should have known he was gay then Mam, he spent the next day crying over the matching sixteen piece dinner plates! (LAUGHTER).

Well, what else to tell you about my Dad. Where's a son supposed to start? Especially when at fifteen that Dad decides to 'come out' to me. (LAUGHTER) I was pretty taken back I have to admit. 'Meet Mike' he'd said. 'He's my fiancée.' I thought; great he's lost the plot. No warning, no handbag carrying or pinkie ring wearing just; 'here you

go son I'm gay, and we're getting married' (LAUGHTER)
So, in all seriousness you can imagine how difficult it was
to get my head round, especially when my head was getting
kicked in for it. (AWKWARD GASPS) To say I didn't
take the news well was a big understatement, I mean I
pushed Mike into an on coming car! (LAUGHTER AND
APPLAUSE) Well, that was the rumour going about. It
was an interesting stag do, wasn't it boys? Location: A and
E, Entertainment: waiting to see if Mike had lost three or
four hundred pints of blood! (SMALL LAUGHTER) but it
all turned out for the best, I mean I came to grips with the
whole gay Dad thing and then the shit (sorry for the bad
language Nan's) (LAUGHTER) asked me to be best man.
And here we are today.

As most of you know, Dad's sudden, in fact, very sudden
transition from Jack the lad to complete monogamist came
as a massive shock to pretty much everyone who knows
him and to everyone that knows me. (LAUGHTER) And
one huge lesson I've learnt since Dad and Mike have been
together is; you really get to know who your real friends
are and who truly means the most to you. And I felt it was
very important to thank every single person who has not
only stuck by me and my family, because lets be honest we
haven't had the easiest of times lately, but for helping us
making our family bond that much stronger. (APPLAUSE)
Because, and even though it's a set up that's not the
average two point four children, God, imagine us all on
holiday – how the hell d'you explain us to a Buntlines
resort? (LAUGHTER) Anyway, what I'm trying to say is;
we've got far more, than most and I'm not talking about the
token gay couple or the very handsome teenager,
(LAUGHTER) I'm talking love and unity and each others
backs! So guys, next time I get my head kicked in you
bunch of idiots (I'd like to call you worse but I've got too
much respect for my Nans) better be behind me!
(LAUGHTER) So, I nearly forgot I'd also have to give

those people, a shout out who cant be with us today for legal reasons, who've made my bones that much stronger, well done! (LAUGHTER) I'm thinking about ditching rugby for boxing (LAUGHTER)

So, apart from teaching me to fight, Mike and Dad's situation has taught me a couple of life's big lessons, one of which being that love really does show up in many different forms. I mean, who's to say what's right and what's wrong when it comes to love? Who made the rules that the 'norm' is heterosexual, now I'm not saying it's a world I'd like to be a part of, that's my girlfriend Kaleigh there next to Mike! (LAUGHTER) but seriously, who cares? If you find love, with whoever it may be, grab it and keep it cause in the words of Shania Twain; 'Looks like they made it, look how far they've come now..' (COUGH) 'Baby, I'm glad they took the *bloody* long way, knew that they'd get there one day!' (LAUGHTER)

Anyway, back to the serious stuff...

Finally, I would like to say another thank you to everybody for coming and joining the newly married couple in their celebrations. And I am sure you will agree they make a fantastic, if not odd couple.

Ladies and Gentlemen: please all join me in a toast.

To the happy couple; long may their love last.

'R Darfod.'

'The End

For more good books like this one,
by a variety of talented authors, log
on to:

www.wugglespublishing.co.uk

Lightning Source UK Ltd.
Milton Keynes UK
27 September 2010

160432UK00001B/13/P